Anna saw a dark shadow flicker between cornstalks.

She spun around and plowed through the stalks. Each of her frantic steps was met with a rustling off to her right. Stalks whacked her face. *Please help me, Lord.* Sensing she was losing ground, she spun back around to face her potential attacker.

Two strong hands gripped her upper arms. A bloodcurdling scream died on her lips when she glanced up to find Eli's concerned gaze on her.

"Someone..." Anna swallowed hard. "Someone was in there."

He pointed to the house. "Go wait up there while I check it out."

Anna nodded and jogged to the house.

After what seemed like forever, Eli strode toward her. "I didn't see anything." He narrowed his gaze. "What exactly did you see?"

"I don't know. Maybe I was imagining things. Maybe I'm as paranoid as my brother."

"No, your brother was worried about you." He glanced back toward the fields. "Until I figure out why, I want to keep an eye on you."

ALISON STONE

left snowy Buffalo, New York, and headed a thousand miles south to earn an industrial engineering degree at Georgia Tech in Hotlanta. Go Yellow Jackets! She loved the South, but true love brought her back north.

After the birth of her second child, Alison left corporate America for full-time motherhood. She credits an advertisement to write children's books for sparking her interest in writing. She never did complete a children's book, but she did have success writing articles for local publications before finding her true calling, writing romantic suspense.

Alison lives with her husband of twenty years and their four children in western New York, where the summers are absolutely gorgeous and the winters are perfect for curling up with a good book—or writing one.

Besides writing, Alison keeps busy volunteering at her children's schools, driving her girls to dance and watching her boys race motocross.

Alison loves to hear from her readers at Alison@AlisonStone.com. For more information please visit her website, www.AlisonStone.com. She's also chatty on Twitter, @Alison_Stone.

PLAIN PURSUIT

ALISON STONE

HTM **HARLEQUIN**® LOVE INSPIRED® SUSPENSE

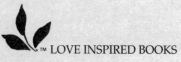 ™ LOVE INSPIRED BOOKS

Recycling programs
for this product may
not exist in your area.

ISBN-13: 978-0-373-44543-1

PLAIN PURSUIT

www.LoveInspiredBooks.com

Printed in U.S.A.

Then Peter came to Him and asked, "Lord, how often should I forgive someone who sins against me? Seven times?"

"No, not seven times," Jesus replied, "but seventy times seven!"
—*Matthew* 18:21, 22

Thanks to my awesome agent, Jennifer Schober,
who stuck with me on this long and winding road
to publication. Your faith in me kept me going.

Thanks to Allison Lyons, my editor,
who championed my work from the beginning.
I'm thrilled we finally get to work together.

Thanks to my fabulous critique partners
and good friends, Amanda Usen and Barb Hughes.
You guys always keep me on track, especially
when I get carried away with the suspense and
forget that it's a romance, too. To Roxanne,
I miss your insightful critiques and sharp wit.

Thanks to Professor Karen M. Johnson-Weiner,
who generously answered my questions about the
Amish. Any errors I've made are mine alone.

Thanks to my mom and dad for providing a
childhood home filled with lots of love and laughter.
Thanks for making financial sacrifices to send
all five of your children to wonderful schools.
It laid the foundation for all my successes in life.
Thank you for that gift.

And thanks to my husband, Scott,
and our four children, Scotty, Alex, Kelsey
and Leah. If you want something badly enough and
you're willing to work hard, dreams can come true.
Thanks for helping me make my dream come true.
I love you guys, always and forever.

ONE

The pungent odor of manure and smoldering wreckage clogged Anna's throat. As she coughed, she tented her hand over her eyes to shield them from the lowering sun. Stalks and stalks of corn swayed under brisk winds, masking the point of impact where the single-engine plane plummeted into the earth. An unmistakable desire to scream overwhelmed her. She clamped her jaw to quell her emotions. She had to hold it together for now. Swallowing hard, she tried to rid her mouth of the horrible taste floating in the air. Across the country road from her parked vehicle, first responders fastened the straps to secure the crumpled plane to a flatbed truck.

Turning her back, she flattened her palms against the window of her car. She closed her eyes as the world seemed to slow to a crawl. Tears stung the backs of her eyes. Her brother was dead. She was alone.

Anna turned around and leaned back against her car. She ran a hand across her damp forehead. It was unusually hot for early October in western New York. The heat rolled off the asphalt, scorching her cheeks. The bold blue numbers *977* stood out on the tail of the plane, remarkably unscathed among the heap of metal. Her brother had sent her a photo of the plane a few weeks ago. He had been so proud of his purchase. She had thought he was crazy. Pressing a hand to her mouth, she realized she had never responded to his email. She had been so wrapped up in her job as a high school counselor at the start of a new school year. Now it was too late to tell him anything.

Her brother had always been there for her when it truly counted. Now only one thing remained for her to do. She closed her eyes. *Dear Lord, please welcome my brother into Your arms.* A tear tracked down her warm cheek.

"Anna Quinn." A male voice sounded from behind her. Swiping at her wet cheeks, she glanced over the hood of her car, surprised to see a tall gentleman striding toward her with a confidence normally reserved for those in law enforcement. Her legs felt weak and she took a deep breath to tamp down her initial trepidation. His dark suit fit his broad shoulders impeccably but seemed out of place among the uniformed first responders dotting the countryside. The intensity in his brown eyes unnerved her.

"Yes, I'm Anna." Dread whispered across the fine hairs on the back of her neck, but she kept her voice even. Her brother was dead. How much worse could it get? Foreboding gnawed at her insides. Past experience told her it could always get worse.

"I'm Special Agent Eli Miller." She accepted his outstretched hand. Warmth spread through her palm. Self-aware, she reclaimed her hand and crossed her arms tightly against her body. Thrusting her chin upward, she met his gaze. The compassion in his brown eyes almost crumbled her composure. She wondered fleetingly what it would be like to take comfort in his strong arms. To rely on someone besides herself.

Heat crept up her cheeks when she realized he was waiting for some kind of response. "You called me about the crash," she said.

The call was a blur, yet she had recognized the soothing timbre of his voice. She had barely gotten the name of the town before she hit End and sat dumbfounded in the guidance office where she worked sixty miles away in Buffalo. She had left without explaining her emergency to anyone in the office.

Anna's chest tightened. "How did you know to call me?"

The deep rumble of the flatbed truck's diesel engine fired to life, drawing the man's attention. The corners of his mouth tugged down. "Your brother asked me to call you."

Anna wasn't sure she had heard him correctly over the noise of the truck as it eased onto the narrow country road. She tracked the twisted metal of her brother's plane on top of the flatbed truck until it reached the crest of the hill. Then she turned to face him. Goose bumps swept over her as the significance of his words took shape.

"When...?" She hesitated, her pulse whooshing in her ears. Had she misunderstood? Was her brother in a hospital somewhere? A flicker of hope sparked deep within her. "When did Daniel ask you to call me? My brother's... dead?" Rubbing her temples, her scrutiny fell to his suit, his authoritative stance. The world seemed to sway with the cornstalks. "You told me he had been killed."

Concern flashing in his eyes, the man caught her arm. "Yes, I'm sorry. I didn't mean to mislead you. Your brother died in the crash." He guided her to the driver's side of her vehicle and opened the door. "Here. Sit down."

Anna sat sideways on the seat, her feet resting on the door frame. "When did you talk to my brother?" She stared at the agent's polished shoes, trying to puzzle it all out. Finally, she met his eyes. "Was he in trouble?"

"Your brother and I talked last week." Special Agent Eli Miller rested his elbow on the open door. "Daniel told me to call you if anything should happen to him." He seemed to be gauging her expression for a reaction.

Anna scrunched up her face. "If *anything* happened?" She pointed to the field. "Like if he was killed in a plane crash?"

"I don't think he could have predicted that, but yes, he asked me to call you." He reached into his suit coat pocket and pulled out a worn business card with a familiar logo on it. She straightened her back. Years ago, after she had landed her first job as a high school counselor, she had dropped the card into a care package for her brother stationed in Iraq.

"Daniel gave you that? I don't understand." She rubbed her forehead, wishing she could fill her lungs with fresh air—air without this horrible smell.

"He wasn't only worried about his own safety." He never lifted his pensive gaze from her face. "He was worried about yours."

"*My* safety?"

"Has anything out of the ordinary happened lately?"

Anna bit her bottom lip. Her mind's eye drifted to the strange note she had found on her car after school last week. She shrugged. "Someone left a note on my car. It was nothing." She struggled to recall the exact words on the note. "I think it said, 'You're next.'"

"Did you report it?"

Anna laughed, the mirthless sound grating her nerves. "No…I'm a high school counselor. A few faculty cars had been egged the week before. That's all it was." She scooted out of the car and brushed past him, turning her back to the crash site. "I took the job to help kids. If I ratted them out every time they looked at me sideways, they wouldn't trust me." Goodness knew where she'd be if her high school counselor hadn't reached out to her.

"Anything strange besides the note?" The concern in his voice melted her composure.

Tears blurred her vision and she quickly blinked them away. "Other than the occasional disgruntled student—who is harmless, I can assure you—I live a pretty boring life."

"Is there anyone you want me to call for you?"

"No," she whispered, staring over the cornfields. An uneasiness seeped into her bones. Her brother tended to be the paranoid one, not her. But she couldn't dismiss it. History told her things weren't always what they seemed. "Can I see your credentials?" Anna met his assessing gaze; flecks of yellow accented his brown eyes. She turned the leather ID holder over in her hands. *Special Agent Eli R. Miller.* It seemed legitimate.

"You met my brother in person?" She studied him, eager to read any clues from the smooth planes of his handsome face. She wanted to ask: Did Daniel seem okay? Was he thin? Dragging a hand over her hair to smooth the few strands that had fallen out of her ponytail, she was ashamed she didn't know the answers. Ashamed she had grown estranged from her big brother. *Dear Lord, please forgive me. Let me find peace through this nightmare.*

Special Agent Miller hiked a dark eyebrow. "Yes. We talked briefly a week ago. I had some questions concerning his return to Apple Creek."

Anna jerked her head back. "I don't understand. He was in Apple Creek working on his photography. Why would the FBI be concerned about my brother's whereabouts?" Foreboding mingled with the acrid fumes hanging in the air.

"Your brother went to Genwego State University, right?"

"Yes." She furrowed her brow. "He dropped out his senior year. What does that have to do with anything?"

"I'm working a cold case. I've been re-interviewing people who lived in the area ten years ago."

"Was my brother able to help you?"

"No. But when I met with him, he was worried about his safety and yours. I had a sense he was somewhat relieved I had contacted him."

"Do you think I'm in danger?"

They locked eyes. He seemed to hesitate a moment before saying no.

She reached into her car and pulled out her purse. She dug out a new business card. Holding it between two fingers, she offered it to him. "May I trade you?"

He accepted the new card and handed her the old one. She flipped it over. In her handwriting on the back she had written: *I'm only a phone call away.* The faded ink was water-stained, but the message was clear. Yet the phone calls between her and her brother had become few and far between.

As she slipped the old business card into a pocket of her purse, the clip clop clip of what sounded like a horse reached her ears. She froze as a horse and buggy made its way along the country road. A man in a brimmed straw hat gently flicked the reins, urging the horse on. Tipping his hat, he seemed to make direct eye contact with the FBI agent as he passed.

Outlined against the purple and pink hues of the evening sky, the buggy maintained its steady progress until it crested the hill and disappeared. Anna made a full circle, taking in her surroundings, including the vast cornfield that greeted her brother's demise. She had been so focused on the crash site—on her distress—she hadn't noticed a neat farmhouse at the top of a long driveway across from the cornfields. A white split-rail fence ran the length of the property. A buggy, the same style as the one that had passed, sat next to the barn a hundred feet or so from the house. The early-evening shadows muted the details, but she realized something she had missed in her distracted state. "An Amish family lives here."

Special Agent Miller nodded, seemingly unfazed. Obviously he wasn't likely to miss such specifics. Besides, he had been in Apple Creek before now.

"My brother's plane crashed on an Amish farm? Ironic." A nervous giggle escaped her lips. "The very community that shuns most technology has one of man's modern marvels plummeting to earth on their soil."

Awareness heated her face when she found him regarding her with a quizzical look. "I'm sorry. I tend to talk too much when I'm upset." Her gaze drifted back toward the crash site, hidden by the tall cornstalks. "Thank God no one on the ground was hurt."

Special Agent Miller nodded but didn't say anything. His economy of words wore on her patience. Fisting her hands, she resisted the urge to slug the information out of him.

Crossing her arms, Anna narrowed her gaze. It wasn't beyond a law enforcement officer to lie to get what he wanted. She had learned that the hard way. "Why are you really here, Special Agent Eli Miller?"

The pain in Anna's eyes spoke volumes despite her display of false bravado. Eli refused to add to her burden, but his conscience didn't allow him to flat-out lie, either. "As I said, your brother's name came up in regard to a ten-year-old cold case." The words rang oddly distant in his ears. This wasn't exactly *any* case.

"Is…was—" she quickly changed tense "—Daniel in some kind of trouble?" Her pink-rimmed hazel eyes pleaded for the truth.

"Ma'am." A baby-faced police officer emerged from the cornfield carrying a green garment. "I understand you're the deceased's sister." Nodding, Anna's eyes widened. "This was in the plane." He held out what looked to be an army jacket.

She grabbed the garment and hugged it to her chest. "Thank you." The officer tipped his hat, respectful of her loss.

"We need someone to identify the body." The officer tapped his fingers nervously against his thigh.

Anna dropped her head and covered her mouth with her hands. "I don't know…."

"Where's the sheriff?" Eli asked. "I thought he'd be out here."

"No, sir, I'm handling this one." The officer tucked his thumbs into his belt and looked at Anna. "We really need you to identify the body, Miss Quinn."

Growing impatient with the officer's insistence, Eli stepped forward, partially blocking Anna in a protective gesture. "I knew the deceased. I'll do it."

Anna lifted her head. "This is something I need to do." Her voice broke over the last few words. "Where…?" Her gaze drifted toward the cornstalks as if she imagined traipsing through the field and finding her brother's bruised and battered body on the ground.

The officer's wary gaze moved to Eli, then back to her. "The morgue is at Apple Creek Hospital. I can take you. It's getting dark and it's easy to get turned around on these country roads."

"Let me drive you." Eli placed his hand on her trembling arm.

Anna nodded, the corners of her mouth pulling down. "Is it okay if I leave my car parked on the main road?"

Eli took her keys, their fingers brushing in the exchange. Anna's eyes snapped to his and he smiled reassuringly. "Let me move your car off the road."

After he moved her vehicle, he guided her with a hand

at the small of her back to his SUV parked in the Amish family's yard. No one was outside the neat farmhouse. Just as well. He had all the information he needed for now. The officer in charge had informed him no one on the ground had been hurt in the crash. *Thank God.*

Eli opened the car door for Anna. Her long lashes brushed her porcelain skin as she ducked into the vehicle. With his hand still on the door handle, his focus drifted to the familiar farmhouse. A young girl emerged from the house, her pale blue gown rustling around her ankles as she sprinted across the grass toward the building next door. The Amish girl reached the neighboring house without so much as turning her bonneted head. Longing for a simpler life filled him.

Squaring his shoulders, Eli strode around the front of the vehicle. The case he was working on had never been easy. The death of Daniel Quinn was an unexpected complication. But even though he was dead, Eli still had to get answers. For the family. For himself.

TWO

"So, Special Agent Eli Miller, what cold case did you talk to my brother about?" Anna had waited until her FBI escort had pulled out onto the road. For a moment back at the farmhouse he had seemed slightly distracted, as if he had something more on his mind than the plane crash. Her shoulders sagged. She squeezed her purse in her lap and held it close. Tears blurred her vision.

He flicked a gaze in her direction, then turned his attention back to the road. "Call me Eli, please." His mouth curved into a small smile, transforming his profile from the serious FBI agent to someone…well, someone not so serious. She ran her pinkie fingers under her eyes. She wasn't partial to men in law enforcement, but her emotional state made her vulnerable to a handsome man with a friendly smile regardless of his chosen career.

Heat crept up her neck and she turned to stare at the cornfields rushing by outside the car window. Instinctively, she was leery of those in law enforcement. Yet Eli's eyes radiated warmth, a kindness, so unlike her father's penetrating glare when he was looking for an excuse to punish her. She blinked a few times to dismiss the memory.

"Are you going to tell me about this cold case?" Anna asked again.

Eli seemed intent on staring straight ahead at the road. "The cold case stemmed from an old case—a five-year-old Amish girl was kidnapped from Apple Creek." His knuckles whitened on the steering wheel.

"Did they ever find her?"

"No." The single word came out clipped.

"Why did you talk to my brother?"

"He was a student at nearby Genwego State at the time."

"You contacted him just because he was a student at the time?" Anna shifted in her seat to look at him directly, fingering the locket on her necklace.

"When the child disappeared, a lot of college fraternities were in Apple Creek doing a pub crawl." A muscle worked in his jaw, but he kept his full attention on the road. "You know, when they come into town and go from one bar to another? Back then at least five bars dotted Main Street. All but one have closed down since. We hoped someone might have seen something."

"Ten years later?" Disbelief edged her tone.

Eli nodded. "It happens. Sometimes someone remembers something they didn't think was important at the time. Did Daniel ever mention the incident to you?"

She shook her head, scrambling to remember. "Ten years ago…I was starting college. That's the fall Daniel dropped out and enlisted in the army. He never mentioned anything about an Amish girl's disappearance. Should he have?" Her stomach hollowed out. At the time, she had found it puzzling her brother had quit college so close to graduation, but he assured her he had a plan.

"Well—" Eli adjusted his grip on the steering wheel "—let's take one thing at a time." He didn't say it, but she knew what he meant. Right now, she had to identify her brother's body.

Anna slumped into the leather seat and leaned her head

back. Before long, the silos, barns and cows were replaced by neat homes and sidewalks as they approached the center of Apple Creek. The last bit of sunlight lit the trees, whose leaves had turned a crimson red and yellow, providing a picturesque landscape. If the circumstances of her arrival had been different, she might have enjoyed the scenery.

Eli slowed his vehicle at a stop sign. Churches occupied two of the four corners of the intersection. Her mind drifted for a moment and she wondered if her brother had maintained his faith after all these years. He had been the one to first drag her to church when they had ended up in a foster home. In church she had found peace and comfort despite the turmoil surrounding their lives.

Silently she said a prayer, asking God to give her strength to deal with the task at hand. Closing her eyes briefly, a quiet calmness descended on her. When she opened her eyes, she noticed hitching posts in front of several of the stores on Main Street. Only one space was actually occupied by a horse and buggy. How peculiar to live as if from another time. Despite having lived in the Buffalo area her entire life, she had never realized the Amish had settled in the countryside little more than an hour away.

Eli drove a few minutes longer, then flicked on the directional and turned into a driveway marked by a large *H*. The small-town hospital was merely a single-story brick building that might have been mistaken for a school if not for the hospital sign out front.

Sensing Eli's gaze, Anna laced her fingers and twisted her hands. In a few minutes she'd have to identify her brother's body. Graphic images formed in her mind. "I don't know if I can do this."

"Come on." He pushed open his door. "I'll be with you the entire time." He came around to her side of the vehicle and helped her out. Streetlamps chased away the gathering dusk.

"Why are you doing this for me?"

"Because it's the right thing to do." With a hand to the small of her back he guided her toward the hospital. Each and every detail—the chipped paint on the bench, the no-smoking sign, the fallen leaves littering the sidewalk—came into sharp focus, as if she were witnessing it all from above.

The automated glass doors whirred open. A sterile, disinfectant-like scent assaulted her. A gray-haired lady in a pink jacket lifted her gaze in mild interest. Eli flashed his credentials and the elderly woman nodded without saying a word.

Eli strode toward a door marked Stairs and opened it for her. "Down one flight." Anna's shoulder brushed his broad chest as she scooted past him into the stairwell. A cool draft floated up from the floor below, sending a chill skittering down her spine.

"I'll be with you the entire time," Eli reminded her, placing a reassuring hand loosely on her waist.

The clacking of her heels on the linoleum became the focus of her attention. Not Eli's comforting presence. And certainly not the task waiting for her.

Reality in the form of a white placard with black lettering slapped her in the face. Morgue. She sucked in a quick breath, then swallowed hard. Nausea licked at her throat.

When they approached a second door, Eli caught her wrist, stopping her in her tracks. Suddenly, she was hyperaware of his touch, the intensity in his gaze. "You don't have to do this. I met your brother. I can identify him." The sincerity in his brown eyes weakened her resolve.

She opened her mouth, then snapped it shut. She glanced

at Eli, then back at the door leading to the morgue. "I have to do this. Daniel's my brother."

Eli nodded. "Okay." His hand slipped down to hers. He gave it a squeeze but didn't let go. The small gesture gave her comfort. "Are you ready?"

Anna turned toward the morgue entrance, then back toward Eli. His features softened and the beginning of a smile tipped the corners of his mouth. The shield around her heart shifted a fraction. She had been alone for so long that she didn't know how to rely on anyone.

"Let's go." Eli pushed open the door leading into a large room. The legs of the stainless steel tables came into view. Her focus shifted from the table legs to the gray linoleum at her feet. Cool, heavy air floated along the floor, licking at her ankles. Eli ran his thumb gently across the back of her hand. "Ready?"

Closing her eyes, she filled her lungs. Would anyone ever be ready to identify a loved one's body? An image flickered across her brain. Her beloved mother, her long blond hair cascading over the pillow in the casket. The beautician had tried her best, she really had, but no one could do her mother's makeup as well as her mother. She used to sit at her vanity every morning perfecting her hair and face, wanting to look beautiful for Father.

The mere thought stirred old fears and insecurities. Anna let go of Eli's hand and crossed her arms. She drew her shoulders to her ears, trying to shake the chill.

"Anna?" Eli's concerned voice broke through her trance. From one nightmare to another. Slowly, she opened her eyes. She forced herself to lift her eyes to the form draped in a white sheet. Her lips thinned into a straight line and she stifled a sob. Out of the corner of her eye, she noticed Eli nod to the only other man in the room. He peeled back the sheet, revealing her brother's face. Bright fluorescent lights cast an unnatural pallor on his whiskered jaw. Darkness pushed on the periphery of her vision. Her heart raced.

Dear Lord, get me through this. Give me strength.

Anna slid her gaze across her brother's features, allowing a numbness to dull the ache in her heart. Her brother's cleft chin, the subtle bump in his nose—the one she shared—and the flat pane of his forehead. Cold, hard reality set in. Her big brother was dead.

Buzzing filled her ears. All the colors came into sharp focus. Blinking a few times, she struggled to concentrate on her brother through her watery gaze, knowing this would be the last time she'd ever see him. Tonight she'd sign the paperwork to have the funeral home pick up his body for cremation. *Dear Lord, help me.* After she cleaned out his apartment, she'd go back to Buffalo and inter him next to their mother.

"It's him," she croaked out. "That's my brother, Daniel Quinn." She turned and buried her face in Eli's shoulder and cried, really cried, for the first time since she had received the news.

"Okay. It's over now." Eli made a soft hushing noise next to her ear, smoothing his hand down her hair.

"I'm sorry." Anna lifted her face and brushed at her tears. Heat burned her cheeks. She had no business seeking comfort from this man. An FBI agent. A stranger. Cupping her cheeks, she stepped back.

"Let's get the papers signed and get you out of here," Eli said.

After Anna took care of the paperwork at the morgue, Eli guided her up the stairs to the main lobby. Before they reached the exit, a clamor came from down the hall. The double doors leading to another part of the hospital swung open, then bounced off the wall. A tall, well-dressed man strode in. His facial features contorted in obvious pain. He held on to a woman at her waist. Her wailing and sobbing scraped across Anna's already fried nerves, and she froze by the stairwell to let them pass.

"Beth," the man cooed in the woman's ear. He ran a hand down her blond hair, pulling it back from her face. "Please," the man pleaded, apparently unsure of how to handle the woman's grief.

Eli put his arm around Anna's shoulders and pulled her close. It seemed the most natural thing to lean into him. To accept the comfort he was offering. "Let's get you out of here," he whispered.

The woman stumbled forward. A groan escaped her lips. As her companion guided her toward the exit, her unfocused eyes drifted to Anna and Eli. Her head snapped up. "Who are you?" Her words slurred as if she had been drinking. She slapped at the tears trailing down her cheeks, wearing off her smooth foundation.

"I'm sorry. I don't think you know me. I'm not from Apple Creek." She struggled to keep her voice from shaking. Eli's grip tightened around her shoulders.

"You're *his* sister." The coldness in the woman's eyes chilled Anna to the bone.

"I'm sorry…." Anna swallowed hard, confusion clouding her brain.

"Mrs. Christopher," Eli said, "now is not the time."

"Get out of my face." The woman pinned Eli with her steely gaze. The two apparently knew each other. With lightning speed, the woman reached out and brought her palm against Anna's cheek with a resounding smack. "Your brother dragged my baby onto that plane. She wasn't supposed to be there." A tear dripped from her quivering chin.

"Mrs. Christopher, please, everyone is hurting here." Eli tucked Anna behind him.

Anna's mind whirled as she stood dumbfounded, her hand pressed to her stinging cheek. Her mouth worked but no words came.

Mrs. Christopher's eyes narrowed into hateful slits. "My baby girl is in there." She jabbed her long manicured finger toward the double doors but didn't turn her head. "They don't know if she's going to make it."

"I am so sorry." Anna's chest grew heavy.

"You will be," the woman said. "I will make sure of it. Your brother was reckless. He had been drinking. Someone saw him at the diner with a beer. *Before* he took my baby up in his plane."

Anna's heart stuttered. She struggled to catch her breath. The conversation seemed to wind down in slow motion. She slipped her hand around the crook of Eli's arm, grateful for the support.

Eli led her past the grieving couple. The man—speaking for the first time—hollered after them. "Special Agent Miller—" disdain evident in his tone "—I suggest you keep Miss Quinn away from us. Her brother has destroyed my family." He lowered his voice. "It would be best if she took care of her business and left Apple Creek immediately. Our family has suffered enough without her here as a constant reminder."

"I wish Tiffany well," Eli said, his voice tight. "Miss Quinn has experienced a terrible loss of her own. If you'll excuse us."

Anna locked gazes with Mr. Christopher. Fury shot from his eyes. The fine hairs on the back of her neck prickled to life, convincing her if she didn't leave town, he'd make her wish she had.

Outside the hospital's main entrance, a black limousine straddled the ramped pavement. Tom Hanson, the driver, leaned against the hood and read the newspaper under the artificial light, seemingly unaware he was being observed. The Christophers were the only people pretentious—and rich enough—to have a chauffeured limo in Apple Creek. Mr. Christopher had created a cable-industry empire and located it in his hometown. The company had satellite offices all over the East Coast but kept their main headquarters in rural Apple Creek. Eli suspected they enjoyed the "big fish in a small pond" cachet it afforded.

Despite Beth and Richard Christopher's angry display in the lobby, Eli's heart ached for them. All the money in the world couldn't buy them happiness if their family was ripped apart. He hoped Tiffany pulled through.

Once inside his vehicle, Eli shifted in his seat. The yellow light from the parking lot lamppost cast Anna's face in deep shadows. "Are you okay?"

Anna's pink lips pulled down at the corners. "Did you know about the poor girl who was on the plane with my brother?" An accusatory tone laced her question.

"Yes." Tense silence hung heavy in the air.

"Why didn't you tell me?"

"I didn't want to burden you."

"You couldn't hide it from me forever." A dark line creased her forehead. "I know you don't know me, but I'm not a fragile woman. Don't hide anything from me. Not when it concerns my brother."

Eli glanced toward the main entrance of the hospital but didn't say anything. Tom opened the back door of the limo and the Christophers disappeared inside.

"How did those people know I was Daniel's sister?"

"Probably because you're with me."

Covering her face, she sighed her frustration. "Don't they realize this is the last place I want to be? There's so much I need to do before I can go home."

Eli reached across and touched her delicate hand, drawing it away from her face. He was secretly pleased when she didn't pull away. "I can help you."

"Why would you help me?"

Because your brother is the last solid link to Mary's abduction. He turned away, afraid he'd chase her off if he told her the truth. He stared at the SUV logo emblazoned on the center of the steering wheel until it blurred. "I'll be in town for a few weeks. I'm here if you need me." He met her gaze.

Anna nodded, skepticism evident in the delicate lines around her eyes. Tipping her head back against the headrest, she yanked the rubber band from her hair, allowing her chestnut hair to fall in loose curls over her shoulders. For the briefest of moments, he wondered if her hair felt as silky as it looked. "Can you take me back to my car?"

"Sure." Tugging at his tie with one hand, he turned the key in the ignition with the other. They drove through the center of Apple Creek. Most of the businesses were closed for the night. When they reached the country road, his headlights cut through the blackness. Silence stretched between them as Eli struggled with how much he should tell Anna about his suspicions regarding her brother. Daniel was dead, so nothing could hurt him now. But what about Anna? She seemed fiercely loyal to him. He wrapped his fingers tightly around the steering wheel. She had suffered enough for today. From what he knew of her childhood through his investigation into her brother, she had suffered enough for a lifetime.

He'd tell her the truth tomorrow.

When they finally reached the crash site, Eli turned into the driveway rutted with wagon wheels and horse hooves. Anna's car was parked on the lawn where he had left it. Sighing heavily, she tucked a strand of hair behind her ear. "Where is the nearest hotel?"

They glanced at each other and a slow smile spread up her pretty face, no doubt anticipating his answer. "Um, all the way back in town." Eli laughed.

"Exactly what I thought." She lifted her hair from her forehead and held it there. Her shoulders slumped. "I just want to grab something to eat and go to sleep."

"What about staying at your brother's apartment?"

Anna shook her head. "I'm not ready to go there. Not yet." She lowered her voice. "That would mean facing all his…stuff."

Eli's eyes drifted to the outline of the farmhouse. "I need to stop in here. Then we can figure out where to grab a bite and a place for you to sleep, okay?"

Anna jerked her head back. "Isn't it too late to drop in unannounced?"

"Come on." He got out and met Anna around the front of the vehicle.

A cool breeze blew her hair softly around her shoulders. Only a hint of the scent of burning wreckage clung to the night air. She hooked a strand of her hair with her pinkie and slid it away from her face. The bright moon lit on her hesitant features. "It seems really late. Maybe we shouldn't bother them."

"Watch your step." He held out his hand and Anna put her slim hand in his. "Come on. It's fine." Her cheek brushed against his shoulder as they navigated their way across the uneven lawn. A clean scent of coconut from her hair drifted to his nose.

Slowing his pace, he reached down and boldly tipped her chin toward the sky. "I bet you don't see those in the city."

"Wow, I don't think I've ever seen so many stars." He stole a glance at the wonder in her eyes and bemoaned the circumstances surrounding their meeting. Another time, another place, perhaps. "There seems to be a certain peace out here. No traffic noise. No nothing."

Eli wrapped his hand around the smooth railing leading up the steps. "It is a peaceful existence. A lot of work. No modern conveniences. But the Amish don't clutter their lives with a lot of distractions. The Amish have a saying, 'To be in this world, but not of this world.'"

"Are you sure this can't wait until morning?" Anna whispered. "Don't they go to bed early?"

"It's only eight-thirty."

"I know, it's just…" She let her words trail off.

"You're uncomfortable."

Anna scrunched up her nose. "I've never met anyone who's Amish." She glanced down at her clothes. "I mean, am I dressed appropriately?" She lowered her voice to barely a whisper, and she tugged at the cardigan covering her sleeveless top. "And I was really hoping to freshen up soon. Do they have indoor plumbing?"

Eli laughed. If only she knew. "Yes, they have indoor plumbing." He gestured toward the window where a soft glow emanated. "And lights. You won't have to fumble around in the dark. They're just not hooked up to the grid."

"The grid?"

"They don't use electricity. But there are plenty of other independent sources of power."

Anna seemed to consider this for a moment. "It's incredible, really, that people still live this way."

Eli leaned on the railing. "We won't be long. I just want to make sure they're okay."

Her tired gaze drifted to the street. The moonlight glinted off her vehicle's windshield. "Okay."

He rapped on the door before she could change her mind. Who was he kidding? He had to do it before *he* changed his mind. Sweat slicked his palms. The door opened slowly.

Beautiful brown eyes met his. A smile broke wide on the woman's face. "Abram! Abram!" she called, glancing over her shoulder. "Come quickly."

Out of the corner of his eye, Eli sensed Anna watching him. He was glad for the shadows. He yanked his tie out of habit as the space suddenly felt close. The door swung all the way open. The woman's long gown rustled in the evening breeze. The hair poking out from under her *kapp* seemed grayer than he remembered. Her bright eyes met his. Covering her mouth, she stepped onto the porch, the kindness in her eyes familiar.

"Eli, you're home."

THREE

Anna watched transfixed as the Amish woman welcomed them. Eli's lips curved into a small smile, but a hint of hesitancy flickered in his eyes. "Anna, this is my mother, Mrs. Mariam Miller."

"Hello, Mrs. Miller. Nice to meet you." Anna did a horrible job hiding her surprise.

"Please call me Mariam." She took Anna's hand in her callused one. "Welcome." His mother glanced over her shoulder. "Your father must be in the barn with Samuel." She spun on her heel. "Let me get him."

Eli reached out and caught his mother's arm. "Wait. How are you? The plane crash this morning must have been a shock."

Mariam fidgeted with the edge of her cape. "Those poor people. Do you know how they are?"

Anna's cheeks grew warm.

"I'm afraid the pilot died. His passenger was the youngest child of the Christophers, Tiffany. She's in the hospital." Eli placed a reassuring hand on the small of Anna's back.

"Oh, dear." His mother's eyes grew wide. "Katie Mae does some housekeeping for the Christopher family. I wonder if she knows...."

"I can talk to her if you'd like," Eli said.

"I hope we're not stopping by too late." Anna found herself studying the space, suddenly fascinated to find herself inside an Amish home. Two oak rocking chairs sat in the middle of a room with wall-to-wall oak hardwood floors. The wood continued halfway up the wall and stopped at the chair rail. The room had a scarcity of knickknacks. Her mind's eye flashed to the assortment of crystal trinkets her mother had collected with reckless abandon. Her childhood home had never lacked for *stuff.* A lump formed in her throat and she pushed the thought aside.

"I'm glad you came." Soft frown lines accentuated Mariam's mouth. "Did the plane crash bring you here?" She gathered her apron in her hands. "The noise. It was horrible." Tears filled the corners of her eyes.

"Yes, I'm afraid it did." Eli momentarily found Anna's hand by her side and gave it a quick squeeze. Anna held her breath, relieved he didn't explain that her brother was killed in the crash. In her exhausted state, she feared any outpouring of sympathy would send her crumbling.

"Do you need a room for the night? I could check with your father. I'm sure under the circumstances it would be acceptable." Mariam stepped deeper into the entryway and called, "Katie Mae, please come here."

"I don't want to cause any trouble." Eli slipped his car keys into his pocket.

Mrs. Miller seemed to study her son's face. "I suppose your brother Samuel won't mind having a bunkmate." She hesitated a fraction. "You weren't planning on sharing a room?"

Embarrassment flushed Anna's cheeks. She imagined that the Amish views on premarital cohabitation ran toward the conservative. "We're not…" She glanced at Eli for help, but apparently they didn't know each other well enough to have their signals worked out.

"My brother was piloting the plane that crashed." She swallowed hard. "I just met Eli today." There, she said it out loud. The reality of her words crashed over her. Biting her lower lip, she hoped to keep her emotions at bay.

Mariam's eyes grew wide. "I am so sorry. Do you need to contact your family? The Jones family down the road has a phone."

Anna closed her eyes briefly. She couldn't find the words to say she didn't have any family. Not anymore. "It can wait," she lied.

A hint of confusion flashed across Mariam's face. Eli's shuttered expression gave nothing away, yet something niggled at her brain. Why hadn't he asked about her family earlier?

A young woman, probably in her late teens, appeared in the hallway. She had on a calf-length dress in a beautiful shade of blue that matched her eyes. Her flawless skin was untouched by makeup. A loop of brown hair poked out the side of her bonnet. The strings on the bonnet dangled by her chin. When her eyes landed on Eli, she smiled broadly. She covered the distance between them in a few short steps and wrapped her arms around his neck. Her cheeks blushed a pretty pink and she quickly stepped back, running her hands down the front of her dress. "Hey, big brother." Her eyes sparkled.

"Hey, Katie Mae."

"So nice to see you. I just got home from work."

"Still working for the Christophers, I hear."

Katie Mae rolled her eyes. "Yes. I'm supposed to do light housework, but half the time I'm watching the grandchildren. They are a handful."

A small smile lifted the corners of Eli's mouth. "I'm sure you handle them just fine." He hesitated a moment, as if weighing his next words. "I imagine it was a little chaotic over there today."

"Oh, dear, yes. Thank goodness Tiffany wasn't killed in that horrible plane crash. Mrs. Christopher is beside herself. Her mother didn't even know she was on the plane until the sheriff showed up at her door to tell her about the crash."

"How horrible," Anna said.

Eli made the introductions between the women, then turned to his mother. "So, Father's still out working in the barn? It's getting late."

"He and Samuel are checking on Red." Katie Mae's voice grew quiet. "He's getting old."

"I brought Red, an Irish setter, home when he was a puppy." A faraway look settled in his eyes. "Must have been more than twelve years ago."

"Why don't you show Anna the extra room upstairs?" Mariam motioned to her daughter. "I'll go discuss the arrangements with your father."

Katie Mae led Anna up the wooden stairs to a bedroom down a short hallway. "Can I get you anything?"

Anna glanced around the tidy room. The furnishings were sparse but clean. A beautiful quilt in shades of blue and green covered the bed. A lone calendar was tacked to the wall. "This is fine. Thank you."

"The bathroom is at the end of the hallway. I will put some clean linens on the chair." The young woman's blue gown rustled around her ankles, revealing black laced boots. "If you'd like, I'll make you some tea and a little something to eat."

"Thank you."

Katie Mae paused at the door, and curiosity lit her face. "Is my brother courting you?"

Anna shook her head. "Oh, no. We just met today."

The young woman frowned. "Too bad." She shrugged. "He could use someone in his life. He's too tied up in his job... Well, your tea will be downstairs." She turned on her heel and disappeared, leaving Anna mildly amused by the question.

Anna flopped down on the bed and closed her eyes. She nearly groaned when she remembered she'd have to retrieve her suitcase from her car. She had packed for a week, knowing she'd have to take care of her brother's apartment in Apple Creek and other details.

"Are the accommodations okay?"

Anna sat up and adjusted the hem of her shirt. Eli leaned on the door frame, a strange look on his face. He had shed his suit coat and rolled his white shirt sleeves to his elbows. Realizing she was staring, she dropped her gaze.

"Oh, man, you're a lifesaver." She stood, relieved to see her suitcase at his feet.

"I try." He stepped into the room, brushing past her, and set the case on the trunk at the foot of the bed. She was keenly aware of him sharing the small space. "I still had your car keys from this morning." Eli tossed them on the dresser. "I'll let you get settled." He turned to leave.

"Wait."

He paused in the doorway and glanced over his shoulder.

"I appreciate all you've done for me today." She held up her palms. "Including this room. But tomorrow I'll go to the motel, because I really don't think I could stay at my brother's place. It would just be too hard." She bit her lower lip.

"One day at a time." The kindness in his eyes warmed her heart.

She tilted her head, studying him. "You grew up here? You're Amish?" She blurted out the questions on the tip of her tongue. She had no right to be intrusive, but she couldn't help herself.

Smiling, he pivoted on his heel. Dark whiskers colored his square jaw. "There is nothing to tell. I was born into the Amish community, but I am not Amish. I left before I was baptized."

Anna narrowed her eyes. "And your parents are okay with that? I thought if you left, you were shunned for life or something."

Eli stepped back and leaned against the windowsill. He undid the knot of his tie. Pulling one end, he unlaced it from his collar, then he ran the silky material through his fingers. "They tolerate the occasional visit, but I'm careful not to overstay my welcome. I don't want to cause them any trouble." He looked like he wanted to say more but didn't. "My parents were disappointed I didn't choose to stay. All Amish parents dream of their children accepting their way of life."

"But it wasn't for you?"

He folded the tie accordion style and gripped it in one hand. He looked up and met her gaze. "It's complicated." He crossed the room and adjusted the brightness on the lamp. "Do you have everything you need? There should be a flashlight in the drawer, too."

Unable to hide her amusement, she shrugged.

"A few less modern conveniences than you're used to?"

"How'd you guess?" She arched an eyebrow.

"The light is fueled by a propane tank in the nightstand."

Anna jerked her head back, marveling at the ingenuity.

"Are these accommodations okay with you? I didn't want to offend my mother when she extended the invitation. I think you'll find it far more comfortable than the Apple Creek Motel." He stuffed his hands into his pocket and crossed his ankles.

"It's fine. Thanks. Really, you've been too kind."

He pulled out his cell phone. "You won't get reception

here, either. If there's someone you need to contact at home, a boyfriend, maybe, we can go to the neighbors. I don't mind driving you." Was there a glint of expectation in his eyes, or was she imagining it?

"No. There's no one." A pain stabbed her heart and she sat back down on the edge of the bed. Then realizing how pathetic she sounded, she added, "I'll update work next week."

"I'm sorry about your brother," Eli said. "It's hard to lose someone close to you." He spoke the words as if from experience, but she figured she had pried enough already tonight.

"I can't believe he's gone." She ran her hands up and down her arms. "I dread going to his apartment. It's going to be hard to pack away his things." Once again tears burned the backs of her eyes. "My brother had called me a few times recently, but I never called him back." Her voice cracked.

Eli left his perch at the windowsill and sat next to her on the bed, pulling her hand into his. "Take it one day at a time."

Their eyes locked. An emotional connection sparked between them. The walls of the bedroom seemed to close in on her, and she closed her eyes to stop the swaying. Exhaustion was catching up with her.

"I avoided my brother's calls because I couldn't deal with him and the demands of my job. He seemed so different after the war. Paranoid. I used to tell him he reminded me of Mel Gibson in *Conspiracy Theory.*" She ran a shaky hand over her mouth. "Remember that movie?" She bowed her head. "I'm so ashamed. I spent my life helping the students at school but I couldn't take five minutes to answer a call from my brother."

"Don't beat yourself up. You didn't know." He squeezed her hand.

Her mouth twisted in skepticism. "But if I hadn't avoided him, I *would have* known something was wrong. Now I'll never have another chance to talk to him. To tell him I love him."

Bowing her head, she covered her face and fought her emotions. Eli placed his solid hand at the back of her head and pulled her into his chest. Sitting on the edge of the bed, she settled into his arms. A mixture of laundry detergent and his aftershave filled her senses.

"Eli—" Anna sat upright. A man with an unkempt beard and blunt-style haircut stood in the doorway "—I need to talk to you downstairs." His cool manner and stare tightened Anna's gut.

"Father," Eli said, his tone even, "nice to see you. This is Anna Quinn." He turned to Anna. "My father, Abram Miller."

The man gave her a curt nod. "If you'll excuse us, I'd like to talk to my son in private."

After his father left, Eli angled his head and brushed his thumb across her cheek. "You okay?"

Anna forced a smile. "You better go talk to your father."

A man of few words, Eli's father descended the stairs and headed outside to the porch. Eli flinched when the screen door slammed against its frame. He caught his father's profile against the backdrop of the night sky. His father was a commanding figure and Eli knew he'd talk when he was ready to talk.

With work-worn hands wrapped around the rail, his father stared out into the distance toward the crash scene. "I never understood man's need to fly. It seems to go against nature." He hesitated a moment before adding, "I pray the man is in God's hands now."

Eli bowed his head. It had been a long time since he had said a prayer. Not so much because of disbelief, but because of apathy, distraction and his job. He scrubbed a hand across his face. Wasn't that part of the reason why his parents—and the entire Amish community—set themselves apart? So they wouldn't be distracted by the outside world and instead could focus on God? Under the night sky, the fields seemed to stretch forever. The Amish believed the agricultural life was as close to God as you could get.

"Anna's brother died in the crash." Eli leaned back in the rocker. The wood felt cool through his thin dress shirt. His grandfather had made these chairs when Eli was a boy. He had been fascinated watching his grandfather work.

"Your mother told me." Abram faced his son, his features heavily shadowed. "But you have been in Apple Creek often over the past month."

"Yes, but never overnight. I drove back and forth to Buffalo." Eli was reluctant to share too much information with his father. They lived in different worlds. "If our staying here is going to cause problems, I'll take Anna to the motel in town."

Abram lifted his hand. "I suppose the bishop will understand the circumstances surrounding your *temporary* stay." His emphasis was not lost on Eli.

"Thank you." He wrapped his fingers around the smooth arms of the rocker. "How did you know I've been in town recently?"

"Isaac Lapp mentioned he saw you in town." *Figures.* The same age as Eli, Isaac had been courting his sister, Katie Mae, almost ten years his junior. Isaac had left Apple Creek to work on a ranch out west years ago, only to return to fully join the Amish faith about eighteen months ago.

His family owned the Apple Creek General Store in town and had welcomed him back with open arms.

And Isaac liked to talk.

"You're chasing a ghost." Abram's statement startled Eli. His father never asked about the investigation that had consumed Eli for the past ten years.

"I have new leads."

"You need to let your sister rest."

My sister. Ten years ago, his sweet sister Mary had disappeared while in town with him. She was only five at the time and he was eighteen. She had been his responsibility. Guilt and anguish sat like rocks in his gut. "I can't."

Under the white glow of the moonlight, his father's eyes flashed. "You are wasting your life. You need to forgive the man who did this."

"You say you have forgiven him, but you have not moved on. Last time I stopped by, you were still leaving Mary's chair empty at the table."

"Your mother…" His words trailed off. Eli waited for his father to continue, but he didn't.

"Dat…" The word felt strange on his lips. "I didn't come here to fight. I came here because I have unfinished business."

"Your unfinished business is a constant, painful reminder to your mother of everything we have lost. We need to have faith and trust in God that Mary is now in His care. Does Anna know you are investigating her brother?" Abram's pointed words hit their mark.

Eli looked up with a start, then glanced toward the screen door. "Did you hear that from Isaac?"

"Isaac had told me to keep an eye on Daniel Quinn because he had been taking photographs in the area." Abram pointed to the cornfield across the way. "This is the same man who died today?"

Eli nodded.

Abram's hand dropped to his side. "Daniel spent a lot of time taking photographs. Claimed they were for a book or some magazine or some such. He seemed respectful. He only took photos of the property. He knew we didn't want to be photographed." Abram fingered his unkempt beard. "Isaac thought we should be aware of who was wandering our property."

Eli scratched his head. "Who else knows I am investigating Daniel?" His mind raced with the implications.

"No one else in the family as far as I know. I told Isaac not to scare the women with his gossip. The next time Daniel had come around, I had asked him to please respect our privacy. I thought it best he not take photographs on our farm anymore."

"How did he respond?"

"He complied. He was always polite. Seemed like a sincere young man," Abram said. "I can't believe this man hurt a child. I am reluctant to believe Isaac." His voice grew low. "It's hard to comprehend such evil."

The pain in his father's eyes tore at Eli's soul. His father rarely mentioned his youngest daughter, Mary.

Eli glanced toward the door, hoping Anna was still upstairs. "Father, we can't discuss this now. I don't want to jeopardize my investigation."

Abram crossed his arms over his chest and leaned back against the railing. "You have not chosen our way of life, but I raised you better than this."

"I am not going to stop looking for the truth." Frustration and anger warred for control.

"Truth?" Abram's bushy eyebrows shot up. "Then don't lie to Daniel's sister. Tell her your suspicions."

"I only met her today. I owe her nothing." The harsh words scraped across his nerves. Had he become so single-minded in his focus that he had lost all sight of others' feelings? Anna's trusting eyes came to mind. It had always been about finding the person who hurt Mary. He never imagined his prime suspect would have a family of his own who might be destroyed by his investigation.

Eli softened his tone. "You'll never understand my choices, but there are things I have to do for my job."

His father's lips drew into a straight line. The Amish were not selfish people. They didn't make choices based on personal preferences and desires. They made decisions for the good of the entire community.

He met his father's gaze. "I have to do it for Mary."

FOUR

Dressed in sweats, a T-shirt and a hoodie, Anna stuffed her feet into her running shoes and tiptoed downstairs. A recurring nightmare had her up before dawn and she thought she'd go crazy inside the small confines of the sterile room. No television, no radio, no electronics. Nothing to distract her. She opened the front door, surprised to find it unlocked. Stepping onto the front porch, she took in the Miller's barn and the dense foliage on the surrounding hills. The first hint of pink colored the sky. The sun hadn't yet poked out over the trees.

A quiet rustling made her glance over her shoulder at the house. For all she knew, the Miller women were up preparing breakfast already. The men were probably in the barn doing their early-morning chores. Not ready to face anyone yet, she jogged down the porch steps and stopped by the road to stretch. A soft wind blew across the cornfields, sending a hint of acrid smoke in her direction. A tightness squeezed her chest.

Focusing all her attention on the ground directly in front of her, she tipped her head from side to side, easing out the kinks. Determined to exercise away her mounting stress, she started her jog on the left side of the road, facing traffic. However, she didn't expect to see any cars at this early hour in the country. As her sneakers hit the pavement, she tried to get into a rhythm. But the image of her brother's cold dead body in the morgue seeped into her brain only to be replaced by more graphic images of her dead mother and father.

She pumped her arms harder. The steady incline of the road forced her to concentrate on her breathing, the placement of her feet, her stride. Soon, her thoughts cleared. She crested the hill and sidestepped some horse manure in the road. A horse and open wagon approached. The combination of the brim of his hat and the dim early-morning light shadowed the driver's features. He waved as he passed. Befuddled, she ignored his greeting and kept running, feeling rude.

The first hint of sun became visible over the treetops. Sweat trickled down her temples. Lost in thought, she realized she had gone much farther than she anticipated. Slowing her pace, she looked up and down the long country road. She crossed to the other side to face the nonexistent traffic as she made her way back.

City habits die hard.

When she reached the road in front of the Miller's home, she leaned over and braced her hands on her thighs, trying to catch her breath. She found herself staring at the cornstalks. She glanced toward the quiet farmhouse, not detecting any activity. But surely they were all up by now. Sucking in a quick breath, she stepped off the road into the soft soil. She held out her arm to push aside the cornstalks. Their sweet smell tickled her nose, and she pinched her nose to stop the threatening sneeze.

Pushing her way through the stalks, she realized she should have followed the beaten path made by the rescue workers. When she reached the clearing, she froze. A small crater of dark soil marked the spot where her brother had met his fate. Tiny white dots danced in front of her eyes. Covering her mouth, she backed away as her stomach heaved. Out of the corner of her eye, she saw a dark shadow flicker between stalks. Training her gaze on the form, she sensed her fight-or-flight response kick in.

She spun around and plowed through the stalks. Each of her frantic steps was met with a rustling off to her right. Her heartbeat ratcheted up in her chest. Stalks whacked her face. *Please help me, Lord.* Sensing she was losing ground, she spun back around to face her potential attacker, but she twisted her ankle on the uneven earth and bit back a yelp. Two strong hands gripped her upper arms. A blood-curdling scream died on her lips when she glanced up to find Eli's concerned gaze on her.

"Thank goodness you're here." Her breath came out in ragged gasps.

"I came outside to look for you when you didn't answer my knock on your bedroom door. What's wrong?"

"Were you walking through the cornstalks?"

"No, I just saw you when you lost your footing." He narrowed his gaze. "What's going on?"

"Someone…" Anna swallowed hard. "Someone was in there."

"Are you okay?"

Unable to find the words, she nodded. He pointed to the house. "Go wait up there while I check it out."

Anna nodded and jogged toward the house. Her ankle seemed fine under her weight. She reached the top step and her rubbery legs went out from under her. Dropping down on to the top step, she wrapped her arms around her middle and leaned forward, her eyes locked on the cornfield.

After what seemed like forever, Eli appeared and strode toward her. Her heart rate had returned to normal. "I didn't see anything." He narrowed his gaze. "What exactly did you see?"

"I…" Her shoulders dropped. "I don't know. Maybe I was imagining things." She pushed a hand through her hair. Maybe I'm as paranoid as my brother."

Eli planted one foot on the bottom step of the porch and leaned his elbow on the railing. "You've had a lot to take in." He offered her his hand and she pushed off the step to stand next to him.

"My nerves are shot." Her laugh came out high-pitched and grating.

"Why did you go into the field?"

"I thought it would help me move past this nightmare if I saw the spot where his plane went down." She had always regretted not returning to her childhood home after her mother's murder. "I guess it was stupid."

"No, it's just that your brother was worried about you." He glanced back toward the fields. "Until I figure out why, I want to keep an eye on you."

Anna climbed a step to gain some distance. She didn't know whether she should be flattered or annoyed. "I can take care of myself. I've been doing it for most of my life."

Eli pinned her with his gaze. "Humor me, would you?" When she didn't answer, he added, "Come on. Let's go inside. My mother is making breakfast."

"Mind if I clean up first?" He held open the screen door for her. She ran up the stairs, aware of Eli watching her. Now *he* was worried she was in danger. *Had* someone been following her in the fields? Shards of ice shot through her veins.

Despite the unseasonably warm October weather, Anna threw on a thin cardigan and capris, compelled to cover her exposed flesh. Anything less and she would have felt severely underdressed—disrespectful even—in this Amish house. Besides, she couldn't shake the chill from her encounter in the cornstalks.

When she finally wandered downstairs to the kitchen, she was quickly ushered to the breakfast table. Mother and daughter in their long gowns, hair neatly pinned underneath their bonnets, moved in a practiced rhythm.

"We trust you had a good sleep, Miss Quinn," Mariam said, never once slowing from the hustle and bustle of preparing breakfast.

"Yes, thank you." The lie flew from her lips. It was easy because Eli's mother never met her eyes. Anna rolled her shoulders, trying to ease the kinks in her back. A bead of sweat rolled down her back in the close quarters of the kitchen. The cooking stove gave off immense heat.

"Are you okay?" Mariam's soft voice snapped her out of her reverie. "Please have a seat."

Unable to find her voice, Anna nodded and pulled out the closest chair.

"No, please, sit in this one." The older woman pointed to another chair. Mariam smoothed her hand across the top of the empty chair and slid it back into place.

Anna sat and leaned into the slats of the wooden highback chair. A fragrant aroma wafted from the stove. Her stomach growled. Until then, she hadn't realized she was hungry. A moment later, Eli strolled into the kitchen dressed in blue jeans and a dark-blue golf shirt.

"Feel better?" The intensity in Eli's gaze unnerved her and she nodded. He pulled out a chair across from hers and sat down. The silence stretched between them.

Nervous energy finally got the best of Anna. "I thought I'd drive by my brother's apartment today. Clean out his things."

"I'll go with you."

"That's not necessary." She blurted out the words on reflex, despite knowing he'd insist. "I don't want you to go to any more trouble than you already have."

"I'd like to see if I can find anything at your brother's apartment that might answer why he was worried." Eli seemed to be selecting his words carefully. His mother placed a bowl of scrambled eggs on the table and smiled but didn't say anything. "I have two weeks of vacation. I arranged it yesterday afternoon with my supervisor."

Anna took a small spoonful of scrambled eggs, then pushed them around her plate with her fork. "For your cold case investigation?" Out of the corner of her eye, Anna noticed Mariam watching her son with keen interest. "Why did you have to take vacation for a case? Isn't it part of your job?"

"It's kind of a personal project." Eli's lips flattened into a thin line. Anna flicked a gaze toward his mother standing by the stove.

"Do you think my brother's worries had anything to do with your investigation? It's not likely, right? He didn't know anything." Dread washed over her as they locked gazes, an unreadable emotion in his eyes. Shaking his head, he cut a sideways glance toward his mother. She took a bite of scrambled eggs despite the knot in her stomach.

A teenage boy dressed in a blue shirt, pants with suspenders and a straw hat burst in through the back door. Despite a scolding from his mother, he raced from one window to the next.

"Hey, Samuel, what's going on out there?" The legs of Eli's chair scraped across the hardwood floor as he stood up.

The teenager leaned on the window's ledge and peered out. "There's a big truck with a long pole on it. One of the English is carrying something big on his shoulder and they're coming this way. *Dat* told me to get in the house. To tell *Mem* and Katie Mae to stay put."

Eli strode toward the front door and yanked it open. When Anna reached his side, she was struck by the hard expression on his features. Eli was a formidable man. A cold chill ran down her spine despite the warm breeze.

A camera crew stood a few feet from the porch steps. A well-coiffed woman with a blond bob and a microphone in hand took a step forward, doing a quick check of her shoes as if she had stepped in something. "Can we speak to someone regarding the plane crash?"

Eli glared at her until she lowered the microphone and gestured to her cameraman to turn off the camera. She pointed the mic at Eli. "Do you live here?" She rearranged her lips into a phony smile. "Help us out here. I need some footage for the evening news."

Eli jerked his chin toward the street. "Take footage from the road. This is private property."

"We'd like to interview someone. We're working several angles." The woman persisted. "At first we thought it was a cruel twist that a plane crashed in the middle of an Amish field. Two different worlds colliding." Her lips quirked. "And, I think a lot of people would be surprised to learn of the thriving Amish community in western New York."

"They can read about it in the guidebooks." Eli started to close the door. The woman raised her voice. "We learned Tiffany Christopher was critically injured in the crash. I'm sure you're aware they're a prominent family in this area."

Anna froze and held her breath. She had the sensation of standing on the ocean's edge about to be clobbered by a giant wave. The reporter's focus turned toward her. "I was told the pilot's sister was in town."

Eli held his hand in front of Anna protectively.

"Do you know—" the reporter consulted her notepad

"—where we could find Daniel Quinn's family? His sister?"

Seemingly in an effort to intimidate, Eli moved toward the reporter. "I *asked* you to leave."

The reporter tilted her head. "I thought maybe we could get a comment from the sister. To clear his name."

Tiny white dots floated in Anna's line of vision. "What are you talking about?"

"Mr. and Mrs. Christopher have alleged the man piloting the plane was unstable. That he had suffered from post-traumatic stress disorder and was drunk when he took the plane up with Tiffany on board." The pounding of her heartbeat in her ears nearly drowned out the reporter's allegations. "I understand there was a history of violence in his family."

Panic pierced Anna's heart. She stepped forward and wrapped her hands around the smooth railing for stability. "My brother died in the crash. Let him rest in peace." Tears clogged her throat, making it difficult to speak. She didn't want her family's tragic past splashed all over the news *again*.

"Your brother?" The reporter's eyes lit up, but she obviously already knew who Anna was. "Would you be willing to go on camera?"

The implications ran through her mind. She didn't know anyone in this small town. Maybe if people knew she was here they'd help her piece together what her brother was doing in Apple Creek that had him spooked.

Keenly aware of the camera trained on her, she inhaled deeply. Daniel wouldn't have risked his life by drinking before flying. None of this made sense. She wished she could rewind time. If only she had kept in touch with her brother.

Anna walked down the porch steps and stared straight into the camera. "My brother, Daniel Quinn, died in the plane crash. If anyone knows—" she started over "—if anyone knew my brother, please contact me." After she rattled off the digits of her cell phone number, Eli placed his firm hand on her shoulder. If his touch was meant to be a warning, it came too late.

An internal voice scolded her for announcing her cell phone number on a newscast, but right now she didn't care. She had nothing to lose. Worse case, she'd get a new cell phone number after things calmed down. "I want to talk to anyone who saw my brother early yesterday morning or the night before his flight. Or anyone who had ties to my brother while he was in Apple Creek."

She was desperate to shed some light on his frame of mind. Had he gone off the deep end with his conspiracy theories? Twin ribbons of shame and grief twisted around her heart. Daniel had always looked out for her. He even saved her life when she was twelve years old. Tears burned the backs of her eyes. It was too late for her big brother, but she owed him this much—to clear his name in death.

"Was it a scheduled flight?" The woman's hawkish eyes shifted from hers to Eli's and back.

This time Eli answered. "Neither Miss Quinn nor I have any information regarding the investigation. You'll have to talk to the sheriff." He lifted his chin. "Now, if you'll please respect the privacy of the family who lives here, we'd appreciate it."

The reporter lowered her microphone and offered her business card to Anna. "If you'd like to do a full interview, please call me." She pursed her lips. "I'm sorry about your loss."

"Thank you." A dark part of Anna's heart suspected the reporter took pleasure in other people's misfortune. It made for good news.

Eli's solid hand rested on her shoulder. She resisted the

urge to lean into him for support. After the news crew crossed the road and started filming the crash site, she looked up at him. "Do you think I made a stupid mistake?"

"Sometimes you have to go with your gut."

A mirthless laugh escaped Anna's lips. "You don't know me very well. I'm not one to shoot from the hip."

Seeming to regard her carefully, he rubbed a hand across his whiskered chin. "Will getting answers help you sleep better at night? Bring you peace?"

She searched his brown eyes, feeling an unexpected connection as if he understood her pain. "I hope so," she whispered.

Eli brushed a knuckle across the back of her hand, the motion so quick she thought she imagined it. "You're not convinced?"

Anna shrugged. She turned and climbed the steps, the wood slats of the porch creaking under her weight. Katie Mae appeared in the side yard and placed a wicker basket on the grass. Bending at the waist, she lifted a wet dress and pinned it to the clothesline. Anna stood transfixed as Eli's younger sister completed the chore. Three rows of garments in subtle hues of gray, bright blue, dark blue and lavender weighed down the lines. Something about the simplicity of the chore, the repetitiveness of it, appealed to Anna. Could peace be found in the simple things?

Anna swept a strand of hair out of her eyes. Nothing about her life had ever been simple.

After the commotion outside the Miller's farmhouse, Eli drove Anna to her brother's place. On the drive over, she finally got the nerve to ask the question that had been haunting her since the reporter first brought it up. "You met my brother. He sometimes gets crazy ideas, but he didn't seem unstable, did he? Had he been drinking?" Her voice cracked over the last word. Their father had been an abusive alcoholic.

Eli ran the palm of his hand across the top of the steering wheel, never taking his eyes off the road. "I can't say he was drinking, but he was agitated. He was worried about you."

"It doesn't make sense. Does any of this have to do with your cold case?" Anna was afraid of his answer. No way had her brother been involved with a child's disappearance. But she had to ask.

Eli cut her a sideways glance. "I don't know. He was reluctant to tell me what he knew, if anything. He seemed afraid." She sensed Eli wasn't telling her the entire truth.

The car came to a stop at the intersection. As frustration welled inside her, a sign on the lawn of one of the churches at the corner came into focus. *No Jesus, No Peace. Know Jesus, Know Peace.* Slipping her hands between her knees and straightening her arms, she wondered why she couldn't instinctively shut off her worries and rely on God. Only her faith could get her through this.

Curiosity nudged her. "Growing up in an Amish community, faith was a big part of it, right?" The entire concept fascinated her. "Do you still go to church?"

Anna studied Eli's profile. A muscle worked in his jaw. He gave her a measured stare. "What is the old saying? Don't discuss religion and politics."

"I didn't mean to offend you."

He stared out the windshield. The silence between them grew thick with tension. Obviously she had touched on a sore subject. About a half mile past the center of town, they turned into the driveway of a well-maintained home. Pots of yellow and purple mums lined the porch steps. Large windows overlooked the front yard.

Eli navigated the driveway until he reached the back of the house. He jerked his chin toward a three-car garage and a set of steps hugging one side of the structure. The furthest bay was open. "Your brother rented the garage apartment." He parked and climbed out. Anna joined him around the front of the vehicle.

A man about her brother's age stepped out of the open garage, wiping his hands on a dirty rag. Something flashed in his eyes when he saw Anna. His unshaven face and buzz cut made her think of her brother's appearance when he got off the plane six months ago from his service in the Middle East. The man wore oil-stained jeans and a ripped T-shirt. It appeared they had pulled him away from his work.

"You must be Daniel's sister," he said, his voice gruff. "I'd see the resemblance even if Eli hadn't contacted me to tell me you were on your way." He stuffed the rag in his back pocket. "Sorry. That was horrible what happened to him. I hear my cousin Tiffany's putting up a good fight, though."

Anna's eyelids fluttered. "Oh, I'm sorry. Tiffany is your cousin?"

The man gave her a solemn nod.

"Did you know my brother well?" she asked, eager to get any information she could.

He jerked his thumb toward the steps. "Daniel rented out the garage apartment. He was busy on some photography project." He narrowed his gaze. "I think he was putting photographs together for a book or something. People seem to be fixated on the Amish." He hooked one thumb through his belt loop. "It's beyond me."

"Did he tell you about his project?" Anna asked. Her gaze drifted to Eli, who stood off to the side with his hands loosely crossed over his broad chest.

"Yeah, he seemed eager to wrap up the project and move on all of a sudden. I figured he needed to finish the job to get paid." He rolled his eyes. "There's not much to do in this town."

"Do you have the key?" Eli asked. "Anna would like to see her brother's apartment."

The man reached into his pocket and pulled out a ring filled with keys. "Sure, man."

"I'm sorry I didn't catch your name," Anna said as they moved toward the stairs leading to the second-story apartment.

"Tom Hanson."

Something jogged in her memory. "Did you know my brother from when he went to college in the area?" Something about the way he was staring at her—almost through her—unnerved her.

"A little bit. He and my cousin Chase, Tiffany's brother, were tight." Jangling the keys, he scrunched up his face, thinking. "They were in the same fraternity at Genwego. I wasn't the college type. I went to trade school. I do pretty good as a handyman and jack-of-all-trades for my aunt and uncle."

"Tiffany Christopher's parents?"

Tom nodded. "My mom and Aunt Beth are sisters. My mom married some loser and moved up to Buffalo a bunch of years ago. Aunt Beth and Uncle Richard have always looked out for me."

Anna glanced at the main house, her chest growing tight. "Is this…their house?" She should have thought of that the minute he introduced himself as Tiffany's cousin. She imagined the back door swinging open and Mrs. Christopher emerging, fury in her dark eyes.

Eli smiled gently and mouthed the words, *It's okay.*

"*Doctor* Richard Christopher, Senior, lives here. He's like a grandfather to me. I hang around in case he needs anything." He held up his hands. "Ah, don't worry. I'm the black sheep of the family. It's my Uncle Richard that runs this town. I'm just another one of their servants." He smirked. "Long story." He shrugged. "Actually, I don't mind. It's steady work. Good pay. Not much else going on jobwise in the booming metropolis of Apple Creek." Tom separated a key from the ring. "Here."

Eli took it from him. "We'll keep this. I'll return it in a few days after Anna goes through her brother's things."

Anna's attention shifted to the stairwell leading to her brother's apartment and she suddenly felt light-headed. Eli flashed her a concerned glance and she forced a smile.

"I think I should hold on to that key." A deep line marred Tom's forehead.

"It's fine," Eli assured him. "It's the beginning of the month. Daniel's paid up to the end, right? I'll hold on to the key."

"I guess so." Tom stuffed the key ring back into his pocket.

The wood creaked under their weight as they climbed the steps. At the top landing, Eli had reached out to insert the key into the lock when the door swung inward. Anna's heart plummeted. Eli held out his arm to stop her forward momentum. "Wait here."

She covered her mouth to stifle her shock. Papers littered the floor. A lamp was upended. Couch cushions had been tossed across the small space. Anna's shoulder hit the doorframe, her knees having gone weak, and she fell to the floor.

FIVE

Eli crouched down in front of Anna and helped her to a seated position. Her legs seemed to go out from under her. "You okay?"

Giving him a sheepish smile, she nodded and leaned her shoulder on the door frame. "I felt a little light-headed. I'm fine. Give me a minute."

Eli studied her face, before saying, "Stay here. I'll be right back." He carefully stepped around the items scattered across the floor of Daniel's apartment. He didn't want to destroy anything that might be evidence. A quick canvass told him whoever had done this was long gone. Frustration simmered below the surface. The break-in convinced Eli that Daniel was more than paranoid. With Daniel's death, Eli feared he might never find the truth. He might never know what happened to Mary.

Eli crossed the room to a small desk in the corner. With the eraser end of a pencil, he shifted through the material. Best he could tell, someone had riffled through everything. When he was here talking to Daniel last week, the apartment had been orderly, meticulously so.

A photo of a rundown shed bracketed by two willow trees caught his attention. "Your brother had an eye for photography." He glanced over his shoulder. Anna had gotten to her feet and stepped into the room, her eyes wide, her arms wrapped around her middle. A ribbon of compassion twisted around his heart. He couldn't deny the connection he felt with Anna. He turned his attention back to the desk and examined the photo.

"He loved photography." Her voice held a wistful tone. "It was his escape. It doesn't surprise me that he came to the countryside to capture its beauty."

"What was he trying to escape?" He turned around to face her.

Her features seemed shuttered. "We had a rough child-hood."

He knew about their childhood, at least all the information available in the files. He had dug into Daniel's past during his investigation into Mary's disappearance. But he knew Anna would shut down if he told her he already knew about her tragic upbringing. He'd hoped she'd mention it first. "Anything you want to talk about?"

Lowering her eyes, she shook her head. She waved her hand dismissively. "No one wants to hear a sob story."

"Try me." He rested his hip against the desk and wrapped his fingers around its smooth edge.

She sat on the arm of the couch and braced her hands on her knees. "I'm only telling you this because it might help you understand my brother."

He nodded but didn't say a word.

If her eyes were lasers, she'd have burned two holes in the floor. "When I was twelve, my father shot and killed my mother…then himself." She ran her pinkie finger under her eye. "That's the CliffsNotes version." She clasped her fist in her hand. "My brother has been my only family since. He was my protector. He watched over me in the foster system."

Her jaw quivered, but she shrugged as if it were no big

deal. "My parents' deaths and his years at war shaped my brother. He was quirky—a little paranoid—but he had a huge heart." She met Eli's gaze with watery eyes.

She ran a hand down her ponytail and dragged the end over her shoulder. "Nothing is easy, is it?" Standing, she sighed. "I just want to pack up his stuff, but now—" she lifted her palms "—this mess." Grief etched her features. "It's as if the world is conspiring to keep me here."

"I'm sorry about your family." Eli took a step forward, but Anna held up her palm.

"I'm fine.… It's old news."

Eli nodded. The hurt in her eyes told him it would never be old news.

"Let's just figure this out so I can go home as soon as possible."

"Whatever you want." Eli studied her for a minute. She forced a smile before wandering over to some framed photographs on a shelf above the TV. Turning his focus back to the desk, he tamped down the urge to comfort her. He had a job to do.

Eli noticed a square, dust-free spot where Daniel's computer had been. Something niggled at his brain.

"What do we have here?" Sheriff Chuck Blakely stepped into the room, something crunching under his boot.

"Tom call you?" Eli crossed his arms and strode toward the door. He didn't want the sheriff's interference. Ever since Mary's disappearance, the local sheriff's office and the FBI had not had the best relationship. There were accusations of incompetence and withholding information on both sides long before Eli joined the FBI. A basic turf war. It also didn't help that the sheriff's son was in the same fraternity as Chase and Daniel at Genwego State at the time of Mary's disappearance. All ranks had closed around Blakely's son.

"Yeah." The sheriff released a long sigh. "Looks like someone did a number on this place." The sheriff pointed to Anna. "You're Daniel's sister. The one on the television." His tone scraped across Eli's nerves. The two men had butted heads more than once over the years.

The sheriff scanned the room. "Best I figure, someone knew about the crash, knew the apartment would be empty and decided to break in."

"Daniel hasn't been in Apple Creek long." Anna frowned. "I doubt many people knew where he lived."

The sheriff raised an eyebrow. "Small town. People always seem to know everyone else's business." He narrowed his gaze at Anna. "The bad guys watch the news, too. They take advantage."

Anna's cheeks grew red. She rubbed the hollow of her neck with trembling fingers. "Maybe I shouldn't have talked to the reporter."

Eli touched her forearm. "You only spoke to the news this morning. I'm guessing this happened overnight."

"After what the reporter said…" Anna's words trailed off, seemingly oblivious to Eli's reassurances. "I wanted to know more about what my brother was doing while he was here in Apple Creek."

Sheriff Blakely scoffed and tucked in his chin. "Like I said, Miss Quinn, it's a small town. Special Agent Miller and I have been watching your brother."

Anna's eyes widened. "Why? Is it illegal to take photographs?"

"No," Sheriff Blakely said, "but Special Agent Miller thinks he might have had something to do with the abduction of—"

"That's enough, Sheriff." A knot tightened in Eli's gut. This was not the way he wanted Anna to find out her brother was under investigation. Her glare landed squarely on Eli. "*You* have been investigating my brother? I thought you were interviewing a lot of individuals who happened to be in Apple Creek ten years ago. But you were targeting him."

"Yes, he was under investigation." Eli gritted his teeth, anger pulsing through his veins. Sheriff Blakely was going to destroy what little trust he had established with Anna.

"Your brother had an uncanny tendency to be in the wrong place at the wrong time." The sheriff couldn't keep his mouth shut. "It was only a matter of time before we found enough evidence to arrest Daniel and charge him for the ten-year-old case."

Anna watched Eli with accusatory eyes. Her pulse jumped in her throat. "There is no way my brother would hurt anyone. Never mind a child."

Eli bowed his head briefly, then met Anna's gaze. Out of the corner of his eye, he knew the sheriff was watching him. He'd have to pick his words carefully. "I'm still trying to put all the pieces together. I'm trying to figure out the extent of your brother's involvement." He wasn't ready to tell Anna the missing girl was his sister. He supposed they both had their share of secrets they'd have to reveal in due time.

Eli turned to the sheriff. "I'd like to talk to Anna in private."

The sheriff stood firm, his eyes growing dark. Then they softened. "Miss Quinn, you'll have to file a report of what's missing in your brother's apartment."

"I don't know what he had." Anna's voice was shaky, distracted.

"You'll have to do your best. Stop by the station." The sheriff strode out of the room, leaving Eli to face Anna.

Anna collapsed onto the only cushion remaining on the couch. "There is no way my brother had anything to do with that missing child."

In a haze of confusion, Anna lowered her gaze. A photo of her brother on the end table caught her attention. Her heart lurched, and tears blurred her vision. She reached over and picked it up. He was about twelve and she was nine. They had huge smiles on their faces and leaves stuck in their messy hair.

Thoughts swirling, she set the photo down and fingered the gold lighter next to it. Tingles of realization blanketed her arms. This was her mother's lighter. And the end table used to be in their grandmother's house. Pressing her fingers to her temple, the world seemed to close in around her.

She rose to her feet and brushed past Eli. She heard his voice but couldn't make out the words. Unable to hold back the tears, she ran down the steps and kept going. She twisted her ankle on the loose gravel and quickly regained her footing. When she reached the main road, she turned toward town.

Tears streamed down her cheeks. Her lungs burned as she briskly walked in the direction she had come. She decided she'd call a cab when she reached town, then collect her things from the Miller's home. She'd find a motel room, clean out her brother's apartment and stay away from Eli. He was using her. He couldn't be trusted. *Just like her father.*

Adrenaline tunneled her vision. How could he think her brother had something to do with the disappearance of a child? Life's circumstances made her brother a lot of things but not someone who hurt children. *Never.*

Her limbs went weak when the general store came into view. Swiping at her tears, she stepped off the curb.

Screeching tires sent needles of icy terror coursing through her veins. Out of the corner of her eye she could see a car barreling toward her. Turning away from it, she dove toward the curb and landed with a scraping thud on her left side. A whoosh of warm air lifted her hair as the car sped by. Searing pain shot to her left knee and elbow.

Get the license plate number!

She pushed up on her elbow and winced. Whipping her head around, a pair of designer shoes blocked her view of the departing vehicle. Anna's gaze traveled upward to the woman's shocked face. "Oh, dear, are you okay?"

Anna scooted to a seated position on the curb, her face warm from a mix of embarrassment and pain. She gave her knee a cursory look. Her insides did a little flip. "Did you notice the car?"

The woman tented her hand over her eyes and looked down the street. "I'm afraid not." She pointed to a large window of a ladies clothing store behind her. A partially dressed mannequin stood shamelessly on display. "I was working on the display when I heard tires screeching. All my attention was focused on you lying in the street." She pouted her pink lips. "I'm sorry."

"Are you okay?" A man called as he ran across the street holding on to his straw hat. He held out his hand to help Anna stand. Her knee throbbed when she put weight on it. "What happened?"

"Some guy came flying out of nowhere and almost hit her." The excited woman signaled with her arms.

Anna brushed off her pants, putting all her weight on her right foot.

"Come over to the general store. I'll get you some bandages and you can clean up. We'll call the sheriff." Hooking his thumb in one of his suspenders, the man let his gaze wander the length of her. She assumed he was assessing her injuries.

The sheriff wasn't exactly on the top of her list of people she wanted to call. He had had such a smug look when he accused her brother. She dismissed the image. What could the sheriff do anyway? No one saw the car. It was probably some college kids on a joyride. *And I wasn't paying attention when I stepped into the street.*

Anna took off her cardigan and glanced at her elbow. Little black bits of gravel dotted her scraped-up skin. "Yuck," she muttered under her breath. "Do you have water at the store?"

"Sure, come on." He offered his hand. "Do you need help?"

"I think I'm okay." Favoring her right foot, Anna did her best not to hobble across the deserted street. In her distracted state she had foolishly stepped out in front of the car without looking. Heat swept up her neck and cheeks. What an idiot. She could have been killed.

The man walked ahead and held open the door, bells jangling against the glass. "There's a chair near the register. Have a seat. I'll get you some water."

"Thanks. Um—" she hesitated for a second "—is there a cab company around here?"

A bemused smile curved his lips. "No." He crossed to the back of the store and grabbed a water bottle from the shelf. Handing it to her, he cocked an eyebrow. "I could give you a ride home on my wagon." A twinkle lit his eye. "Unless it's too far."

Anna sat down and accepted the bottle of water. "Thanks anyway. I'll figure something out." She stretched her bruised leg and suddenly second-guessed her decision to run out on Eli.

The man smoothed a hand down his suspenders, studying her. "You're Daniel Quinn's sister." He lowered his gaze. "I'm sorry about the accident."

"Thanks. But—"

"I saw you on TV," he interrupted before she had a chance to finish. He lifted a finger to his lips. "Shhhh... don't tell anyone." He pointed to the front window. "Sometimes I linger over my coffee at the coffee shop down the street so I can watch TV." He leaned back on the counter. "I'm Isaac Lapp. My family owns the store."

Anna twisted off the cap from the water bottle and took a long drink. "Did you know my brother?"

"He came in the store once in a while. I knew him a bit from his college days, too." Isaac shrugged a shoulder. "I was in my running-around days then. We had some fun. But lately, Daniel had been focused on his photography. We didn't have much in common anymore." He flicked the brim of his hat.

"I suppose not." With everything else clattering in her brain, it was outside her imagination to guess how Amish people spent their spare time. She figured they didn't regularly hang out with—what did Eli's brother call them?— ah, the *English*.

The bell hanging from the front door jangled. Eli stood in the doorway, a pinched expression on his handsome face. No doubt the excitable lady across the street had directed him to her whereabouts.

"I bet he could give you a ride in his car." Isaac pointed to Eli. "You know Anna Quinn here? Her brother was the one you've been asking questions about."

Eli closed the distance between them, shooting daggers at Isaac with his eyes. When his gaze met hers, his brows snapped together. "What happened?"

Anna examined her elbow, cognizant of Eli, who had crouched down in front of her, resting a hand on her knee for support. "I wasn't paying attention and stepped in front of a car. It was stupid. I got a little banged up when I jumped out of the way. That's all."

Eli gently inspected her elbow, his warm fingers trailing the uninjured flesh near the pebbles stuck in her arm. Her traitorous heart did a little flip flop. "Did the car stop?" She shook her head. "You get the license plate or a description?"

"I was too busy with my face plant." Anna pulled her arm away and stood up, brushing past him. She yanked the pant leg of her capris up to inspect her knee. Losing her balance, she leaned forward, resting her palm on Eli's broad chest. Their eyes locked and lingered a little longer than she had intended. Fire in her cheeks, she glanced down, focusing all her attention on her knee. It looked pretty much the same as her elbow. Just great.

Anna examined a nearby shelf. "Can I have those bandages?"

"Sure." Isaac pulled out some things from behind the counter.

"Did you see anything?" Eli asked Isaac.

"Nope, just heard the commotion. I was around back taking some boxes to the Dumpster. Sorry." Isaac crossed over to the shelf, grabbed a second water and offered it to Anna. "Maybe you should pour this over your knee. It will clean it up a little until you can get home."

"Thanks."

Isaac took off his hat and hung it on a peg. "Can I get you anything else? Want me to call the sheriff?"

Anna's eyes met Eli's. He was the first to speak. "No, I'll look into it." He wrapped his hand around Anna's waist. "Let's go." Her wounds ached, but they were bearable. "I have a first aid kit in the car."

"Suit yourself." Isaac stepped behind the register. Anna

reached into her purse and pulled out her credit card. Isaac held up his hand. "We don't take credit cards."

"Oh."

Eli opened his wallet and pulled out a twenty.

Isaac waved him off. "Forget about it. I'm just glad I could help."

"Thank you." Anna forced a smile. "I think the sooner I get out of Apple Creek the better. So far I haven't had a very pleasant stay."

Isaac seemed to regard her for a moment as Eli nudged her forward. "How about you, Eli? You plan on hanging around Apple Creek much longer?"

"I have some time off." One side of Eli's mouth slanted into a grin, but the smile didn't reach his eyes.

Isaac pushed out his lower lip, seeming to give it some thought. "I guess I'll be seeing you around." His dark eyes landed on Anna. "I'm real sorry about your brother. You'll probably make arrangements and then be on your way, I suppose." Isaac leaned back and crossed his arms. "Most people don't hang around Apple Creek for long. It's plain too quiet."

"Thank you for your help. I do have a lot to do." The water sloshed out of the bottle as she moved toward the door. "I better go before I make a mess in your store."

"I suppose you won't be looking for that cab anymore." Isaac's words competed with the bells clacking against the door.

With Eli supporting her, Anna hop-walked onto the side-walk. She wheeled around, gritting her teeth against the sudden pain shooting up her leg. She leaned in close, resisting the urge to pound her fist against his solid chest. "You used me to get to my brother." She struggled to catch her breath. Her heart beat wildly against her ribs. "You wanted access to his apartment. You wanted to search his things.

And you couldn't legally do that unless I invited you to come into his apartment."

"I told you at breakfast that I wanted to see if I could uncover anything in his apartment."

"You never told me you planned to use whatever you found *against* my brother."

"I don't want to argue on the sidewalk." Eli cupped her right elbow and guided her toward his SUV parked by the curb.

She yanked her elbow away from his grip. "Someone broke into my brother's apartment. What do you think they were looking for?"

"I don't know." She couldn't read the expression in his eyes. Was he still holding something back?

The tiny hairs on the back of her neck prickled to life when a new, horrible thought took hold. "Do you think his plane crash was an accident?"

He let out a heavy sigh. "I don't know. I called a friend in the FAA to check out the plane."

"Oh, no, this is unbelievable."

"Let's not jump to conclusions just yet." He gently nudged her toward his vehicle again. "We need to clean your wounds so they don't get infected."

The flesh on her elbow was torn up and discolored. Her stomach did that little queasy thing again. "Have you ever done this before?"

"Cleaned a wound?" He slanted her a glance as if to say, "Trust me."

But she didn't trust him. Not by a long shot.

Eli yanked open the back door of his SUV and held out his hand. "Have a seat."

Anna narrowed her gaze and squeezed past him, obviously not ready to forgive him. He couldn't blame her.

Holding on to the door for support, she lowered herself on to the backseat. She grimaced as she examined her elbow. "I think it looks worse than it is," she said.

Without asking her permission, he gently took her wrist and extended her arm. A soft gasp escaped her lips. He poured the water over the wound and she winced. "When we get back to the house, we can do a better job of this."

Anna scratched her head with her free hand. "Maybe I should find someplace else to stay. It will be easier for me to handle my brother's affairs without worrying you'll try to use something against him."

Eli stepped back and rested his elbow on the doorframe. He had totally botched this. Just because they both had painful pasts didn't make them kindred spirits. He sighed heavily. "I'm looking for the truth. Don't you want to know the truth? Even if it hurts?"

Hiking up her chin, a look of determination lit her hazel eyes. "I know the truth. My brother would never in a million years hurt a child."

"You said yourself you had grown apart over the years." He poured more water over the wound.

Anna wrenched her arm free and scowled at him. He held up a hand. "Before you make your case, let me get the first aid kit." He grabbed the white box from the back of the SUV and found her pacing the sidewalk. She flinched every time she stepped on her left foot.

"We may have grown apart, but I know the type of person he is…was." Anna stopped and squared off with him.

"I know you loved your brother, but we don't always know a person's heart."

"I don't believe any of this."

Eli held up the kit. "You gonna let me help you?"

Anna bowed her head and sat back down on the edge of

the seat. She held still as he wrapped her arm with a clean bandage and clipped it in place.

"Pull up your pant leg." Eli twisted off the cap of the second water. Anna held her leg out so he could run the cool water over the wound without getting the inside of the vehicle wet.

"Man, that's cold." Anna shivered. "Tell me, why my brother? I thought there were lots of fraternity guys in Apple Creek that evening." He supported her foot on his upper thigh as he wrapped another bandage around the wound.

As Eli put the clip on the bandage to keep it in place, he sensed her growing unease. She planted her foot on the curb and levered herself out of the car. He grabbed her forearm as she tried to brush past him, but she jerked away. "You weren't on this case in the beginning, were you?" she asked.

"No." He pinned her with his gaze, wondering when she was going to put two and two together and realize the missing Amish girl was his sister. "I took the case over from an agent who retired."

"You're going off his theory then?"

"He was a solid agent." Eli walked around the back of the vehicle and tucked the kit away in his trunk. He rejoined Anna by the side of the car.

Anna crossed her arms and stepped toward him. A soft breeze blew a lock of hair that had escaped her ponytail across her face, sending an alluring scent his way. "How did they narrow their list of suspects?" Her eyes sparked. "My brother made your short list of suspects because the FBI was aware of his troubled past. The FBI knew he had been considered a suspect in my parents' deaths."

Eli nodded. He forced his shoulders back and tried to erect a wall around his emotions. This tactic had served him well over the years as he dealt with tragic cases. But when it came to this case, anger and hurt easily pierced the wall.

Don't make it personal. An emptiness sloshed in the pit of his stomach. That line had been crossed a long time ago when it came to this case.

Yet he owed her some information. "The sheriff and the FBI agent at the time of the child's disappearance did know about your brother's background."

"You're just like the police who initially investigated my parents' deaths. They couldn't imagine that one of their own killed his wife. You knew my father was a police officer, right? He used that authority to control my mother. To control us. After his death, his *brothers* tried to pin it on Daniel, the so-called troubled teen. But you want to know the truth?" She dragged the side of her shaking hand across the bottom of her eye. Her voice wobbled. "He saved my life the day my parents were killed." Anna stared off in the distance. "If he hadn't locked me in my room that day, I would be dead, too."

SIX

Anna stuffed her hands in the pockets of her capris and drew her arms in close. She shuddered, suddenly feeling terribly exposed on the sidewalk in front of the general store.

"Let's get you something warm to drink. There's a coffee shop…" His words trailed off, and she followed his gaze.

"Ah, what do we have here?" Mrs. Christopher glared at them with hardened features.

Eli seemed to regard her for a moment. "Good morning, Beth. How is Tiffany?"

The woman's gaze faltered for a moment. She smoothed a hand down her long blond hair. "My Tiffany is still in a coma, but the entire town has her in their prayers. She *will* get better. It's just a matter of time." She sniffed and angled the sharp lines of her chin. Clutching her purse close to her body, she said, "I wanted to stop and get Tiffany her favorite candy for when she wakes up."

"Glad to hear it," Eli said. "Please let me know if you need anything. Do you still have my number?"

Beth glared at him with disdain. "I don't need anything from you." Her gaze shifted to Anna. "I understand the garage apartment was broken into."

Emotions Anna couldn't quite name narrowed her throat. "Yes, I'm afraid so."

"That's rather unfortunate." Mrs. Christopher seemed to notice Anna's bandage and paused for a moment. She wiggled her fingers and widened her eyes. "It's always something, isn't it? I'll need you to have your brother's things out of the apartment as soon as possible. I have another renter. I can't have people thinking it's empty, an easy target."

"I thought my brother had paid until the end of the month."

Beth flicked her hand in a dismissive gesture. "Daniel had a verbal agreement with my son. I'll gladly refund the balance of his rent." She took a few steps toward the general store and glanced over her shoulder. "Please, clear out his things."

"You've got to be kidding me," Anna muttered, shaking her head. "She's heartless."

"Come on, let's get some coffee."

They walked the block to the coffee shop, ordered their drinks and settled at a table by the window. Anna took a few long sips of her café mocha, letting the liquid warm her insides. "I guess I better clean out Daniel's apartment right away."

Eli reached over and brushed a thumb across the back of her hand. "I'll help you."

She pulled her hand back and placed it in her lap. "How can I trust you?"

"I'm sorry." Eli tapped his thumb on the handle of his mug. "I didn't tell you right away about the investigation because the timing wasn't right. You had only learned about your brother's death."

Looking at the ceiling, she hoped to stop the threatening tears. "I'm tougher than I look." She gave him a faint smile and a tear spilled down her cheek.

"Oh, yeah?"

His playful tone made her laugh. "I don't like to talk about the day—" she lowered her voice to barely a whisper "—my father killed my mother, but…." The need to explain propelled the conversation forward.

"You don't have to talk about it. I read the case files." The compassion in his voice made her resolve slip. He knew all the intimate details of her tragic past. Details she had carefully hidden from everyone in her life. It was easier to shut people out. Pretend she didn't have this horrible past.

Pulling her hands into her lap, she narrowed her gaze at him. "I have to tell you. If I don't, you'll twist it around to use it to suit your case. That's what the police did. I can only imagine how the police reports read. They turned everything around to protect my father."

Anna took another sip, letting the warm liquid flow down her throat. "That night, my mother woke me up when it was still dark out." Outside the coffee shop, a horse trotted by, pulling an open buggy carrying a young Amish woman. She blinked away the blurry image. "Mom had told me to hurry up and pack a few things. She had finally decided to leave my father. I had been begging her to do it for ages. Now that she had finally made the decision, we didn't have much time. My father—" she struggled to say the word without tasting the bile in her mouth "—was due home from the midnight shift soon."

Anna tilted her head from side to side, trying to ease the stiffness between her shoulder blades. Nerves tangled in her belly under Eli's intense gaze. "I got up and threw a few things in a suitcase. Then I heard shouting coming from the kitchen. My father had arrived home early."

Anna's gaze shifted to Eli, then back to the street. It would be easier to tell the story without seeing the concern in his brown eyes. "My father had been pushed over the edge."

"You don't have to tell me any more," Eli whispered in a soothing voice. "I know what happened. It's too hard for you."

She traced a finger along the rim of the cup. "No, the reports don't tell the whole story. The reports were filled out by my father's friends on the force…the good ol' boys club."

"But the truth about your father killing your mother then himself eventually came out."

"The accusations did a number on my brother." She pursed her lips. "The reports can't possibly tell the entire story." Running her fingers through the end of her ponytail, she turned her gaze on him. "That morning, I heard my mother pleading with my father, so I tiptoed into the kitchen." The scene unfolded in her mind like a made-for-TV movie. "My father was yelling at my mother." Spittle shot from her father's mouth. "He told her she had no right to leave. He had something in his hand."

Anna smoothed her hand along her hair, the long-ago day replaying with gut-wrenching clarity. "I was about to confront my father." Her eyes locked with Eli's. "I *hated* my father. He was a chameleon, you know? One minute he was so sweet and the next he'd smack the smile off your face.

"Before I had a chance to confront him, my brother grabbed my arm, dragged me to my bedroom and locked me in. He made me promise I wouldn't try to come out until he came to get me." A shaky breath escaped her lips. "A few minutes later my father pounded on my door. Screamed at me to come out." She ran a hand under her nose. "I heard my mother hollering at him. I slipped into my closet and sat on the floor. I can still see the trim from my dance costume draping down in my line of vision, the walls shaking around me as my father pounded the door. But I didn't come out."

* * *

Anna stared out the window with a faraway look in her eyes. She fiddled with a locket around her neck and her shoulders drooped, as if she were drawing into herself while she retold the details of that horrific day.

"The rest is a blur." She narrowed her gaze as if searching her memories. "I heard my father walk back down the hall, yelling for my brother. I heard a shot, then another." She ran her hands up and down her arms. She finally turned to meet his gaze. Hurt resonated deep in her hazel eyes. "The silence that followed was deafening. I sat on the floor of the closet for an eternity. I thought my brother was never coming back. Finally, I heard a knock. My brother whispered my name through the door." A tear ran down her cheek and plopped on to the table. "I was afraid to unlock my bedroom door in case it was a trick…but it wasn't a trick.

"My father killed my mother, then killed himself. Daniel had tried to stop my father, but he was only a kid himself. When my father threatened to kill Daniel, he had no choice but to hide."

Eli couldn't imagine the terror she had lived through that day. He wanted to reach out and pull her into an embrace, but he hardly knew her beyond the words in a report filed a long time ago. He had successfully kept a professional distance from the people in the tragic reports he read day in and day out. Until today. If only their circumstances were different.

"If Daniel hadn't locked me in my room and hid himself, my father would have killed us all."

"I'm sorry." His words were all he had to offer.

Closing her eyes briefly, she twisted her threaded fingers. "And you think because my brother was exposed to such violence that he repeated the cycle?" The frustration was evident in her voice.

He owed her honesty. "Yes. It's a theory."

"No way. Daniel had been a bit of a hellion when he was growing up. But after my parents died, he was my guardian angel. He protected me the entire time we were in foster care. I would have been lost without him."

Eli slumped back in his chair and ran a hand across his whiskered chin. He had to dig deeper. Get everything out in the open. "There were reports that perhaps your brother had been the one to fire the gun, killing your parents."

"That was all fabricated. The cop who first responded was a friend of my father's." Her eyes glistened with tears. "He tried to get my brother to confess."

"Why did your brother drop out of college?"

Anna shrugged. "I don't think he ever fit in. He decided to enlist in the army. I don't know."

"He dropped out right after the Amish girl went missing." *The Amish girl. My sister.* Eli neglected to tell her that, though. *So much for honesty.* The air was already thick with emotion and he wasn't quite ready to let her see the pain in *his* soul.

"That doesn't make him guilty." Her pink lips curled into a grimace. Suddenly her expression softened and her eyes grew wide. "It makes sense if he dropped out due to the stress of the investigation. Daniel went through a lot when they interrogated him after my parents died. Who would want to go through that again?" She ran a shaky hand across her mouth. "But he never once mentioned anything about this girl's disappearance to me. He must have been worried it would be pinned on him." She bit her lower lip. "Remember how paranoid he could be?"

Eli leaned forward, resting his elbows on the table. "I think Daniel knew something about the child's disappear-

ance." What part Daniel played in it was still up for de-
bate. And now that he was dead, Eli feared he might never
solve the case.

Anna leaned back in the chair and crossed her arms.
"What *exactly* did Daniel say when you met with him last
week?"

"He seemed skittish. He claimed he was in Apple Creek
for a photography project. And like I said, he was worried about his safety and yours. "Eli ran a hand across the
back of his neck. "I knew I'd have to earn his trust before
he talked, so I didn't push. Now I'm afraid it's too late."

"Daniel didn't trust many people." A mirthless laugh escaped her lips. "He came by it honestly after everything he'd
been through. I have no idea why he'd be worried about me. I
live a very quiet life." Her brow furrowed. "However, I have a
had a run of bad luck lately." She shook her head as if dismissing the notion. "Maybe I'm becoming as paranoid as he is."

"I'd like to keep a close eye on you."

Her eyes widened. "No, I'm fine."

Eli held up his hand to quiet her protest. "I believe he
knew something, and now that he's gone, I'd like your permission to search his things."

Red splotches flared on her cheeks. "If I do that, you'll
use anything you might find against him. You don't really
care if he's guilty. You just want to close your case. Gold
star for Special Agent Miller. Move on to the next case."

A muscle worked in his jaw. "Do you really believe
that?"

She arched a brow. "My father was in law enforcement.
He didn't leave me with the best impression of the profes-
sion."

"Someday you're going to have to trust someone. I'm
asking you to trust me."

Anna stilled and stared at him but didn't say anything.

Eli continued. "Ten years ago, Daniel belonged to a fraternity on campus. A couple of the seniors, your brother included, were rumored to have sent a few freshmen on a mission, like tipping a cow. But in their twisted version, it involved harassing the Amish."

"This all ties in with the girl's disappearance?" The color drained from her face.

"The buggy that had transported Mary to town was found about a mile away, overturned in a ditch. The FBI figured something had spooked the horse, sending it bolting away with Mary inside. Sugar—the horse—had to be put down." Eli cleared his throat.

"But what about the child? What happened to her?"

"Never found." Eli fought to keep his tone even. "Last time she was seen was inside the store. No one saw her outside the general store. Perhaps she climbed back into the wagon on her own before the horse was spooked." He rubbed a hand across the back of his neck. "We haven't been able to put all the pieces together."

"But you do think my brother was involved?"

Eli quickly glanced over his shoulder. They were the only customers in the coffee shop. "Yes, but he wasn't the only one."

"Chase Christopher was one of his fraternity brothers." Anna placed both of her palms on the table and sat ramrod straight.

"Exactly."

"That explains Mrs. Christopher's disdain for you."

"I'm good at making friends." He smiled.

"I can see that. So you're investigating Chase, too?" The hope in her voice squeezed his heart. He so wanted to give this woman good news. Something to hang on to.

Eli plucked at the napkin crumpled on the table. "The

Christopher family is very powerful. Mr. Christopher hired the best lawyers for his son."

Anna slumped back in her chair and crossed her arms. "Figures."

"The sheriff's son was also in their fraternity."

"And he was untouchable, too." Anna rested her forehead in her hand.

"The sheriff made it difficult, but the FBI kept pushing. Both Chase and the sheriff's son had rock solid alibis."

"And my brother?" The air grew heavy with tension. "Did he have an alibi?"

"None of his fraternity brothers vouched for him. He claimed he was taking photos by the lake. I fear the truth may have died with your brother."

Anna tilted her head. "I'll help you find the truth. If Daniel was involved with something stupid that went bad, he would have come forward a long time ago. I know my brother."

"People make stupid decisions all the time. They get trapped." Eli snapped his fingers. "And in a flash, one decision, then another changes the course of his life. Then he doesn't know how to go back."

"Even if my brother knew something, he wouldn't have waited ten years."

"It's hard to know what someone would do under pressure." Eli met her gaze and his heart went out to her. How would Anna handle not only the death of her brother, but also the news that he may have been involved in a horrible crime?

"My brother is level-headed under the worst of circumstances. He proved that to me when my father killed my mom. I just can't…" She seemed to be deep in thought. "Wait." She leaned back and dug her cell phone out of her purse. "My brother left me a voice mail a week ago. I saved it. Something about it didn't make sense, but I dismissed it. I thought it was another of his conspiracy theories. He said he was taking photos, working on a new project." She looked up. "He needed help."

"Was it unusual for him to reach out to you?" He leaned forward and tried to read the screen of her cell phone, but it was too far away.

"Daniel never asked for help." She shrugged. "Well, at least not before he went to war. He was always the one who helped me. In the message his voice sounded strained." She twisted her lips. "I dismissed it, figuring I'd deal with it later. I'd had a rough week." She smoothed a hand down her ponytail. "I should have called him back."

She traced her finger along the rim of her coffee mug. "I just wanted to flop on the couch, watch some television and veg out." She lifted her watery gaze to meet his. "You know, I counsel students for a living. When my own brother needs me, I check out."

Eli squeezed her hand but didn't say anything.

She held up a finger in a wait-a-minute gesture. "I have to power the phone up. I turned it off because I wasn't getting a signal at your parents' house." She glanced at him briefly, then back down at her phone. "His voice mail said to check my email. He knew I'm not good about checking my personal email account." After a minute, she clicked on the screen a few times. Her features grew slack and she held out her phone with a shaky hand.

He put his hand under hers for support and read an email message.

Anna ~ tried to send important photos. Taking too long to upload! Will bring them to you. Flying up this afternoon. Some crazy stuff going on. Need to see your smiling face and lie low for a bit. Be safe.
Luv ya ~ D

"Did he try to send the photos again?" Eli's nerves hummed with anticipation.

She flicked her index finger across the touchscreen. "No, no other emails from him." She rubbed her temples. "I wish I knew what he was talking about." She collapsed against the back of the chair, a haunted look on her face. Suddenly she bolted upright. "Did they get everything from the plane?"

Eli nodded.

"There was no luggage? No camera? Daniel said he was going to bring the photos to me."

"No, nothing other than Tiffany's purse. The sheriff already returned it to her father." Excitement buzzed his nerve endings. He understood where she was going with this. Maybe Daniel did have proof. Maybe Daniel had photos. Maybe that's what someone was looking for at his apartment.

"Did you notice a camera in his apartment or maybe from the plane crash?"

"No. Daniel was traveling light. I think they only planned on going up to Buffalo for the day. And I didn't notice his camera in the apartment."

Anna jumped to her feet. "I have Daniel's jacket in my car. Maybe he had a USB flash drive with photos in his pocket." She tilted her head. "It's worth a shot."

Eli's nerves hummed the entire drive. As they crested the hill near his family's farm, he pressed the brake, slowing for a buggy, its orange triangle in stark contrast to the black body, one of the Amish's concessions to a modern world. Two young boys not more than two years of age sat on the floorboards behind the seat, seemingly oblivious to the car following them.

"That doesn't look safe. Look how easily they could fall

out." Anna sounded horrified. A short lip on the platform of the buggy and one black bar about halfway up were the only restraints keeping the boys inside.

"Theirs is not a world of car seats and lawsuits."

"But still," Anna said. Eli watched the one boy reach across and snatch something from the other boy's hand. The second boy seemed unfazed. They wore sky-blue shirts, suspenders and hats. Something tugged at his heart. He missed the simplicity of growing up in this community.

Drumming her fingers on the door, Anna huffed in frustration.

He cut her a sideways glance. "They live and think differently than we do."

"It's not that. I'm anxious to see if Daniel left anything in his jacket."

"I don't want to go around the buggy on this blind hill."

Anna pulled her hands into her lap and twisted her fingers. "I know."

"We're almost there." The Amish woman at the reins guided the buggy a little closer to the side of the road. "I used to hate when a vehicle approached my buggy." Eli flexed his fingers around the steering wheel. "Some of the college kids used to beep their horns and swerve close, hoping to startle the horse."

"Really?"

"We…the Amish—" he quickly corrected himself "—just want to exist peacefully. It's increasingly difficult as the outside world encroaches on their way of life." Eli carefully pulled out and around, giving the buggy a wide berth. He waved in greeting, but the woman on the buggy didn't acknowledge him. A short distance up, Eli turned onto his family's property.

"Where's my car?" Anna leaned forward, straining to see through the windshield, her eyes scanning the horizon. She sagged against the seat. "Oh, that's right, you moved my car."

"Out of respect for my parents. It's acceptable for the Amish to ride in a vehicle even when they can't drive, but my father is pretty strict. And always worried about appearances. No sense setting him off by parking your car in front of his home. Sometimes the neighbors talk." He tipped his head. "Even in an Amish community. They're still human."

"But surely the neighbors would understand it's not their vehicle."

"Yes, but whenever I come around, I try to be discreet. The bishop has suggested to my parents that I may not be a good influence on the younger men in the district. I don't want to cause my parents any additional grief."

"I don't have a childhood home to go back to, either," she muttered. Her voice had a faraway quality that worked on the shield surrounding his heart.

Eli drove his SUV around the back of the barn. The vehicle rocked over the ruts of the narrow wagon wheels. How many times had he ridden the horse and buggy to this point? Then he'd have to take care of the horse. Taking the key out of the ignition and climbing out seemed so simple in comparison. Yet sometimes he missed the steady beat of the horses' hooves, the wind whistling past his ears and nothing on his mind but the task at hand.

"You coming?" He blinked at Anna's voice. She gave him a quizzical look and aimed her key fob at her car. The lights flashed.

Walking alongside the vehicle, he tensed when he noticed the back passenger window was smashed. Pink blossomed on Anna's cheeks and she shook her head.

She peered inside, careful to hold her hands away from the shards of glass clinging to the doorframe. "Daniel's jacket was in the backseat." She straightened. "Now it's gone."

Eli tented his hands over his eyes to block the late afternoon sun. The only thing that broke the endless tract of fields was the occasional farmhouse or barn. In the distance, someone worked the field guiding a team of horses. "I don't get it. No one knew the car was back here. You can't see it from the road." He rubbed the back of his neck. "Unless someone saw me move it."

Anna crossed her arms. "Why would someone steal Daniel's jacket?" She opened the back door before he had a chance to stop her. She reached in and pulled out a piece of paper. She looked up, fear in her eyes. "This note says, 'You're next.'"

Eli's gut twisted. Was someone else looking for the same thing they were? Did someone else know Daniel had incriminating photos? *If* he had incriminating photos. Once again, a potential revelation about his sister's disappearance was pulled out from under him. Something sinister lurked in this town and someone was determined to keep it under wraps.

Daniel's concern for his sister came to mind. "I don't like this one bit." Eli scratched his head. "I think you should go back to Buffalo until I figure out what this all means. I have a couple weeks off from the bureau. I'll continue the investigation. But I want to know you're safe."

"Buffalo isn't that far away. Why do you think I'd be safer there?" Anna flattened her palm against her forehead, her eyes glistening with fear. "This is the same note I had on my car in the school parking lot. The same handwriting. I thought it was a stupid prank from the students."

A long brittle silence stretched between them before Eli spoke. "Daniel was afraid for your safety. Maybe someone had threatened you hoping it would scare Daniel into stopping whatever he was doing."

"What do you think he was doing?"

"I think either he had evidence in the missing child case or he was close to uncovering it."

Anna's eyes brightened. "So this means he's innocent." Her words came out in a rush.

Eli touched her forearm reassuringly. "Maybe. But it could also mean your brother was going to confess and take someone down with him." He slammed his fist against the frame of the door. A section of glass rained down the side of the car. "I don't like this. I'd feel better if you went back to Buffalo. I will have someone keep an eye on you there."

"Why can't you protect me?" A timid smile played on her lips even as tears filled her eyes.

"Oh, come on. I don't have time to babysit you."

Her eyebrows shot up. "Babysit? Are you serious? I can help go through my brother's things. I can help you find whatever it is these guys are after."

"I can't risk that." Eli tilted his head from side to side, trying to ease the growing tightness in his neck. He wanted nothing more than to keep her close. But he couldn't deal with losing anyone else close to him.

"Why come after me?"

"You're Daniel's sister."

Anna held up her palms as if to say "And…?"

"I've investigated many crimes. The bad guys don't always have logical reasons. And unfortunately, sometimes we don't know their motives until after they're caught." Eli opened the back door and examined the inside of her vehicle. Glass littered the back seat and floor. As far as he could tell, the only item they had taken was Daniel's jacket. "Maybe they think you have something they're looking for. Maybe photos?"

Anna's eyes grew wide. "We have to find the photos. I just know they'll prove Daniel's innocence."

Shaking his head, Eli muttered something she couldn't quite make out. "Listen, if you're going to stay in Apple Creek, I want you to stay here at my parents' house so I can keep an eye on you."

"I don't want to bring trouble to your family."

The thought had crossed his mind. "I'll be staying there, too."

Anna shrugged, seemingly resigned. "What now? Do we call the sheriff?"

"No. The sheriff has been a detriment to this investigation. The Christophers are powerful people in this town. I wouldn't be surprised if they have the sheriff under their thumb. And there's the issue of the sheriff's son."

"And Chase Christopher. He's still on your short list of suspects?"

"He had a rock solid alibi, remember?"

"You don't sound convinced." Anna crossed her arms. "It doesn't make sense. If my brother was the fall guy, why make threats against me after Daniel's dead? It only proves that someone else has something to hide."

"I was thinking the same thing." He plowed a hand through his hair. "I'll look into it myself. Tomorrow morning, I'll go back to Daniel's apartment and sort through his things and see if we can find anything. There has to be something there." He pinned her with a gaze. "And they don't want you to find it."

"I'm going with you to my brother's apartment." Her pinched features radiated her distrust.

Eli pulled out his cell phone, then remembering the lack of reception, slipped it back into his coat pocket. "I'm going to drive into town and make a few phone calls. Give me your phone."

Anna furrowed her brow but handed it to him.

"I'm going to program my phone number into your phone in case you need me. But if it's a true emergency, call 9-1-1. They have the capability to track your location if necessary."

"Good to know." Anna's casual words belied the fear in her eyes. "But it's not going to help me out here. There's no cell reception."

"It will be okay," Eli assured her. "Let's get you inside."

They started to walk across the lawn toward the house when Anna caught Eli's arm. "Wait. What about little Mary's family? Maybe one of them is out for revenge. Maybe they hate me because they think my brother hurt their little girl? Wasn't Isaac blabbing around town that the FBI was investigating Daniel?"

"Isaac likes to gossip. But no, it's not Mary's family." His answer came out clipped. Certain.

"No. Just no?" Anna's voice went up an octave. "How can you be sure?"

Eli looked down into Anna's eyes and tamped down the emotion brewing below the surface. "Because Mary was my little sister."

SEVEN

Anna's hand flew to her chest. "Oh, no…why didn't you tell me?" Her mind churned to reframe everything he had told her up to now.

A muscle in Eli's jaw twitched. "I try to maintain some professional distance. It's hard. Most people know my history. Apple Creek is a small town, so I don't have to tell anyone." He pointed toward the barn on his parents' farm. "Let's go in there so we can talk in private." Without waiting for her response, he strode into the barn. Anna had no choice but to follow.

Slits of sunlight streamed in through the walls of the barn, creating pockets of light and darkness. It would be completely dark before long. The earthy smell of hay reached her nose. She was surprised to see a tractor parked in the corner of the barn, its large wheels void of rubber.

"Over here." Eli gestured with an open palm to a hay bale.

Anna sat and the coolness seeped through her khaki capris. Running her fingers along the edges of the bandage on her knee, she waited for Eli to speak. He paced the small space in front of her. "Mary was only five years old the day she went missing." His fists tightened at his side. "My mother had asked me to run into town to get something.

Our family was hosting worship service the next day so everyone was busy with preparations. Little Mary had come running over to me, begging to go along."

He stopped and lowered himself on to the hay bale next to hers. "On the buggy ride into town, Mary was chatty, telling me everything going through her mind." A small smile played on his lips as he talked about his little sister in a wistful tone. Anna's heart ached for him. She reached over and rested her hand on his solid forearm.

"How old were you?"

Eli met her gaze. "Eighteen."

Leaning forward, he rested his elbows on his knees. "I've replayed the events over and over in my head. We went into the general store and she wanted to look at the candy display near the front. I went in back with Mr. Lapp, Isaac's father, and we sorted through the supplies my mother needed for the communal meal."

Bowing his head, he threaded his fingers through his hair. Her hand slipped from his arm. "I don't know how long we were in the back of the store, but when I came out front Mary was gone." Clenching his jaw, he turned away from her. "And so was my horse and buggy."

Anna rested her hand on his back, his strength evident under her touch. "I'm so sorry."

"I should have never taken my eyes off her." Despair dripped from his voice.

"It's not your fault." He flinched.

"I was responsible for her."

For the first time, Anna realized why she was instinctively drawn to this man. They shared a deep pain. He understood the heartache haunting her each day.

The creaking of the barn door hinges captured their attention. Red, the family's Irish setter, ambled in followed by Samuel. Moving directly to Eli, the aging dog pushed his nose onto his former master's lap and was promptly rewarded with getting his ears fluffed. "Hey, buddy. How ya doing?"

Samuel started to back out. "I didn't mean to interrupt."

"No, it's okay," Eli said. "How are you?"

"Good." Samuel shrugged, as if embarrassed. "I was going to get Red his dinner." He gestured to a bag of dog food propped in one of the stalls.

Eli pushed to his feet. "I'll do it."

"Okay, then I'll get cleaned up for dinner." He took a few steps toward the door, then spun back around. "*Mem*'s probably going to be wondering if you'll be staying for dinner."

Eli flicked a glance at Anna. "What do you say?"

Tiny butterflies flitted in her stomach. "That would be nice, thank you." She'd never admit it to Eli, but she hoped to get to know his family a little better, to help shed some light on the type of man he was. Then a part of her wondered why she cared. As soon as she had things settled in Apple Creek, they'd be going their separate ways.

"Hey, Samuel, did you see anyone around here earlier today? Someone broke the back window of Anna's car."

Samuel narrowed his gaze. "No, I was busy in the fields most of the day. We're harvesting the corn for feed."

The somewhat familiar half-smile pushed up one side of Eli's mouth. "Okay. Well, tell *Mem* we'll be in shortly."

Samuel turned and strode out of the barn. "He seems so serious. Is that the Amish way?"

Eli seemed to consider her question for a moment. "He took Mary's disappearance quite hard, too." Eli crossed over to where the dog food was stored. Bowl in hand, he scooped in some of the food. The chore was punctuated by pats and hugs to his beloved pet. He obviously loved the dog. He glanced over his shoulder at her. "Samuel is Mary's twin. They had been inseparable."

Anna's heart tightened. "I can't imagine."

Eli patted Red's head, then left him to eat.

"You miss it here, don't you?" Anna asked.

"Some things, but I could never go back."

A little part of her was relieved. As long as Eli was part of her world, there was hope for more. Yet she feared she was confusing empathy and compassion for feelings of closeness.

"You became an FBI agent to help find your sister's abductor?"

Eli settled back down next to her on the hay bale. "The FBI got involved right after my sister's disappearance. The agent in charge had sympathy for me. I admired him. Not long after, I left home, studied hard and was admitted to college." He ran a hand across his jaw. "It was a long journey. I had a lot of catching up to do. At the time, I only had an eighth-grade education."

"Really?"

"The Amish don't value education the same way we do. They fear it could lead the youth away from their homes." Red noisily slopped up his dinner a few feet away. "The FBI agent pitied me and took me under his wing. The goal of becoming an agent kept me focused. Then working as an agent propelled me forward. Guilt is a powerful motivator. I could have been destroyed by it."

Anna understood guilt. She often wondered how different things would have been if she hadn't convinced her mother to leave her father. Had coming home and finding his family packing been the final straw? Maybe she should have just dealt with it and left home as soon as she turned eighteen. Instead she had embarked upon a campaign to convince her mom to leave her father, not wanting to abandon her. Anna's pleading and her mother's decision had sealed their fate.

"Even though I haven't made an arrest in my sister's disappearance, I've helped a lot of other people along the way." Red strolled over and curled up at Eli's feet. He reached down and stroked his fur. "I guess that counts for something."

Anna brushed the back of her hand across his whiskered cheek. "It counts for a lot."

He reached up and caught her hand in his. Their gazes lingered. Something she couldn't quite name hung, unspoken, between them, softening her heart. A sad smile played on his face in the dim lighting. "I can't rest until I figure out what happened to my sister."

After dinner Anna helped Mariam and Katie Mae clean up the dishes despite their protests that they didn't need any help. Eli had run into town to make some phone calls. She tried not to think about everything that had transpired today. She just wanted a few minutes to quiet her mind. The routine of doing dishes provided that. When the dinner dishes were dried and put away, Mariam invited Anna to join her in the sitting room.

Anna leaned back into the deep rocker and rested her scraped-up leg on a wooden footstool. She had cleaned the wounds out more thoroughly before dinner. Her knee throbbed a little from standing in the kitchen for so long, but other than that she figured she'd survive.

Sitting across from her, Mariam picked up her embroidery. The even up and down of her hand as she worked the needle through the fabric was mesmerizing. The quiet ticking of the battery-powered clock filled the silence. This was such a different existence than the life she lived in Buffalo, where she often had the radio or television on for background noise.

Anna wondered a little guiltily if Mariam knew of the

suspicions surrounding her brother. If she did, she didn't let on. An urge to assure the dear woman her brother had nothing to do with her daughter's disappearance almost overwhelmed her, but she decided not to spoil the mood.

"It's so quiet here. Peaceful."

Mariam nodded. "How are you doing, Anna? You have suffered a terrible loss."

Weariness weighed heavily in her chest. "I'm fine."

Mariam nodded, then examined the design in her fabric. Setting her project aside, Mariam rocked slowly back and forth in her rocker, a faraway look descended into her eyes. "You only met my Eli yesterday?"

Anna gripped the smooth handles of the rocker. "Yes."

The corners of Mariam's pale lips turned down. "That surprises me. I would have guessed you've known each other longer. You seem—" she seemed to be searching for the right word "—comfortable with each other." Mariam waved her hand in dismissal. "I suppose it's just as well…" She let her words trail off. "My heart longs for him to come home."

"To return to the Amish life?" The words flew from Anna's lips before she was able to call them back.

Blushing, Mariam picked up her project and guided the needle through the fabric. "I want to know that he's okay. It would give me a measure of peace." She lifted her gaze to meet Anna's, a plea in her eyes.

The next morning was Sunday. Feeling uncomfortable in his own skin, Eli followed a half step behind Anna up the steps of Apple Creek Community Church. How she picked this one over the church across the street was a mystery to him. He supposed it had to do with the time of the church service.

"I don't know how you talked me into this," he muttered.

"Is this what you and my mother were conspiring about last night? To get me back to church of some kind?"

"No, this is strictly for me." Anna bowed her head, her long chestnut hair flowing in loose curls over her shoulders. "I need to go to church this morning to pray from my brother. Sometimes I get so caught up in the trials of life, I forget to lean on my faith." Her voice cracked over the last few words. Immediately regretting his flippant attitude, he caught her hand and gave it a quick squeeze.

"And to pray for Tiffany's recovery," she added as she pulled on the large wooden door leading into the church.

Eli quickly reached around her and grabbed the wrought-iron handle. She smiled her thanks and brushed past him as they entered the foyer. He realized this was the first time he had ever been in a church building. Growing up in an Amish community, they worshiped in barns and homes, a throwback to the days of fearing persecution.

Anna slipped into a pew at the back of the church. In the quiet moments before the service started, Eli tried to recall one of the prayers he had memorized as a child, but he couldn't focus. He was eager to get back to Daniel's apartment and go through his things thoroughly. Maybe they'd find something they had missed, perhaps the photos.

Anna's shoulder brushed his as they scooted along the polished wood of the pew to make room for another family. He couldn't figure out how this woman he had just met two days ago had convinced him to attend a church service. No other woman had ever had this kind of influence over him. Her long lashes swept her smooth skin as she bowed her head in prayer. She was absolutely beautiful.

And your job is to keep her safe. Period. A harsh voice snapped him out of his daydream. And if the investigation continued on the track he suspected, she'd never forgive him for accusing her brother of hurting his sister. His shoulders sagged and he settled back in the pew.

A sharp clacking drew Eli's attention toward the center aisle. Beth and Richard Christopher strode into the church, her heels sounding against the hardwood floor, their eyes straight ahead. Next to him, Anna's face grew red. "It's okay," he whispered.

"Coming here was a bad idea. I had no idea this was *their* church."

Eli reached over and touched her knee. "I think technically it's God's church."

A quiet giggle bubbled from her lips. Warmth coiled around his heart.

A few moments later, the minister took the altar and led the congregation in prayer. Anna stood silently next to him while everyone around them joined in. When the song finished, the minister greeted the congregation.

"This is a glorious Sunday and we owe much thanks to the Lord. Our prayers have been answered. I have wonderful news this morning about Tiffany Christopher, a young member of our church, who as most of you know had been in a horrible plane crash. She has regained consciousness. Praise God."

Eli's gaze locked with Anna's.

"Please continue to pray for her complete recovery. We welcome her parents here this morning. Let us pray." After a slight pause, the minister added, "Let us also pray for the young man who perished in the crash. I understand he was new to our small town. May he find eternal peace."

Eli waited until the quiet reflection was over before he whispered into Anna's ear. "I hate to do this to you, but we have to go."

A vertical line appeared between Anna's brows, but she

didn't argue. They slipped out of the church. "What's going on?" she asked as soon as they were outside.

"If Tiffany is awake, we need to talk to her right now. While her parents are still in church."

"Do you think they'll let us in to see her?" Anna's insides twisted into knots. Part of her was afraid of what she'd learn from Tiffany about her brother. But deep in her heart, she knew he had nothing to do with Mary's disappearance.

"Yes. I may have to tell them it's official FBI business, but they'll let me in."

"Is it official FBI business?"

"I'm FBI and it's important to me."

Anna nodded and swallowed a lump in her throat, deciding not to force the issue further. "I don't know if I can do this. I'm not very good in hospitals." Her grandmother had already been in frail health when her mother had died, so she couldn't take in her orphaned grandchildren. Less than a year after Anna's mother was killed, her grandmother lingered for three weeks in the hospital before dying.

Outside the ICU wing, Eli cupped Anna's shoulders. "I want you to stay outside the room near the nurses' station. I'll go in and talk to Tiffany." He raised an eyebrow and seemed to try to read her thoughts. "Are you okay?"

Anna waved her hand in dismissal. "Fine. Just not a fan of hospitals." She shrugged. "But who is, huh?"

Eli nodded, pinning her with his intense brown eyes. "We don't know what kind of shape Tiffany's in, so don't count on anything. She may not be able to talk to us."

Anna nodded in understanding. Leaning an elbow on the counter at the nurses' station, she watched Eli approach Tiffany's bed. She had a clear view through floor-to-ceiling windows. The area was filled with quiet chatter, subtle beeping and the occasional squeak of a nurse's sneaker against the shiny linoleum.

Tiffany opened her eyes and blinked a few times when Eli approached. She wore a look of confusion on her pretty face. Anna understood why her brother may have been attracted to her. Tiffany's gaze seemed to drift past Eli and land on Anna. Lowering her eyes, Anna felt like she had been caught gawking. Her heart rate kicked up a notch.

When she lifted her gaze, Tiffany pointed a shaky hand, tubes and tape attached, at her. Eli turned around and nodded. He came to the door of the hospital room. "Tiffany's a bit out of it, but she wants to see you."

"Me?"

"Apparently she recognized you from a photo in Daniel's apartment."

Anna struggled to find words. Eli took her hand and led her into the room. Tiffany lay back on her pillow, her eyes tracking Anna's movements.

A small smile pulled at the corners of Tiffany's mouth.

"I'm Daniel's sister, Anna." Tiffany seemed very frail underneath the thin hospital blanket. "How are you feeling?"

Tiffany's forehead creased. "I'm just glad to be here. Time will tell." The young woman's eyes drifted toward the window. "I'm sorry about Daniel. He was a really nice guy."

"Thank you." Eli stood close behind Anna, providing much needed moral support. "Do you know what Daniel was up to recently?"

Tiffany dragged a shaky hand across her mouth. "He liked to take photographs."

Anna glanced up at Eli. There had to be more to it.

"Was he doing anything more? Was he looking for something?" Eli asked. Anna could tell he was being careful with the questions, but he kept glancing toward the door, making her even more nervous. She wondered how long they had before her angry parents showed up.

Tiffany scrunched her lips. She seemed to be struggling with a decision.

Anna took a risk and covered Tiffany's hand with hers. "You can't hurt Daniel now. Please tell us if you know anything."

The young woman sighed heavily. "He seemed obsessed with the disappearance of Mary Miller. I don't know why."

"He didn't say?" The eagerness in Eli's voice mirrored her own emotions.

"No. I figured he was going to do a feature on the story with photographs."

"How did you meet Daniel?" Eli asked.

"He came by the house looking for Chase, but my brother was out of town. He travels a lot for work." Tiffany rolled her eyes. "The all-important *family* business." She coughed. Eli stepped around Anna, picked up the water from the bedside table and held the straw to her mouth. She took a few sips. "I told Daniel I had an interest in photography and we started hanging out." Tiffany gave them a watery smile. "I thought he was cute and so different than a lot of the boys my mom tries to fix me up with. At first I just lied about liking photography. But his enthusiasm for it was contagious."

"Where were you going on Friday morning?" Anna asked.

"To see you. He was worried. He said you hadn't answered any of his calls. He hadn't taken his plane up in a while. He figured we could take a short trip to Buffalo."

The email suggested he had been flying to see her but having it confirmed made her feel even worse. She crossed her arms.

Tiffany shrugged a thin shoulder. "I tagged along at the

last minute. I thought it would be fun to shoot some photos from the plane. I'm sure my mom was shocked when she learned I had been in a plane crash. I told her I was going shopping with a friend. Once I recover, she'll probably kill me for lying to her." Tiffany laughed.

"I'm sure they're just thankful you're going to be okay." Eli set the cup of water back down on the table. "Did Daniel have his camera with him on the plane?"

"Yes. He never went anywhere without it."

Anna rubbed her forehead, wondering where the camera was now.

"Did Daniel ever catch up with Chase?" Eli glanced at the clock on the wall. The church service would be ending soon.

"Yes. Once he stopped over to see me and Chase was home. They went outside to talk, so I didn't hear the entire conversation. But he was obsessed with something that happened when they were in the fraternity. He wouldn't tell me." Tiffany's voice grew soft. She started coughing again and tears ran down her cheeks. Eli grabbed a tissue from the bedside table and handed it to her. Her cough subsided. "They were arguing. Chase was telling him to leave well enough alone."

"Do you know what he meant by that?" Anxiety sent chills up Anna's spine. Eli had mentioned his sister went missing during the fraternity's rush week.

"Do you know if their argument had anything to do with my sister's disappearance?"

Tiffany's eyes widened. "Goodness, no. My brother is a lot of things, but he'd never hurt someone. Not physically. I know Daniel was obsessed with Mary's disappearance, but I never even considered they might have been arguing about that." She narrowed her eyes. "Chase was going on and on about how fraternity brothers always looked out for one another. He is big into that fraternity stuff. Chase was a legacy. My dad belonged to the same fraternity." Tiffany scrunched up her nose. "If only Chase would be as loyal to me."

"Why do you say that?" Eli handed her a second tissue.

"I went to college and earned a business degree, but Chase edges me out of the family business every chance he gets. And my parents haven't been much help. My father won't address the issue. And my mother has always favored Chase. Must be a firstborn thing."

Tiffany curled her lip. "My mom thinks a worthy career aspiration is to become a trophy wife. Like her. She brags she hit pay dirt when she met my dad."

"What did your parents think about you hanging out with Daniel?" Eli locked gazes with Anna. Anticipation charged the air as she waited for the answer.

"Let's just say he wasn't exactly husband material." Tiffany coughed. "Who cares? We were just enjoying each other's company." She looked up at Anna. "Your brother was a nice guy. He spoke often of you, Anna. It was obvious you guys were close."

They had been close once. Anna put her hand on top of Tiffany's. "Thank you." She gave the young woman a quivery smile. "Thank you," she repeated.

Eli squeezed her shoulder. "We'll let you sleep, Tiffany." He put his business card on the table next to her bed. "Call me if you remember anything else."

Tiffany nodded and then sank deeper into the pillows. "I will."

EIGHT

An oily scent hung in the air at the airplane hangar, reminiscent of the crash scene. Anna drew in shallow breaths and said a quick prayer, hoping the rescue workers had overlooked Daniel's camera or a USB flash drive among the wreckage. If Daniel had brought his camera, like Tiffany said he had, where was it?

When they rounded the corner, the twisted metal of her brother's plane rested on a tarp in the far corner of the hangar. Anna gasped and pressed a hand to her chest. She thought she had been prepared to see it again. Blinking rapidly, she spun around to face the wide opening of the hangar, to take in the brilliant blue sky, to settle her raw emotions.

Eli gently placed a hand on the small of her back and she stiffened. "Why don't you hang back here? I'll search the plane."

Anna plastered on a smile. "I'm fine, really." Her gaze drifted over the twisted heap that was once her brother's pride and joy. Tears burned the back of her nose.

"You don't have to be brave. I'm here." She lowered her gaze to the floor, but when he touched her arm, she was forced to meet the tender look in his eyes. "I can search the plane."

Their gazes lingered for a moment before she closed her eyes and gave him a curt nod. "I have to do this."

"Okay then. We do it together." Eli's hand slid down her arm and his fingers intertwined with hers. "Okay?" he whispered, squeezing her hand. The scent of his aftershave tickled her nose and she smiled, suddenly calmer.

When they reached the wreckage, Eli released her hand. "Let me peek inside." He rested one foot on the metal frame and glanced over his shoulder. "The sheriff said they didn't find anything in the cockpit. They may not have noticed something small like a flash drive if they weren't looking for it. I can't imagine they'd overlook a camera."

Please God, let us find something. Anything. Anna walked around to the other side of the plane and leaned in, resting her hand on the cool metal, almost afraid to touch anything. The hangar was eerily quiet. No one else seemed to be around. Anxiety had her ready to jump out of her skin. Anyone could have had access to this plane. It sat in the middle of an unsecured hangar in the heart of cow country. Had someone else already been poking around? The same person who broke her car window and stole Daniel's jacket?

"Watch the broken glass and sharp metal," Eli said.

She double-checked the placement of her hands, then continued to scan the cockpit. "It could be anywhere." If it existed at all.

The sound of footsteps echoed across the expansive hangar. Anna looked up to see a man walking toward them with a clipboard. Eli greeted him warmly. "Anna this is Tim Gardner with the FAA." Eli turned back to Tim. "I didn't realize you'd make it out here so quickly."

"I did it as a special favor for you." Tim clapped Eli on the shoulder.

"Thanks. Have you had a chance to look at it?" Eli asked.

"Just finished going over it a few minutes ago. Must have

been in the main office when you two strolled in." Tim looked down at his clipboard, then back at Eli. "I'm going to have to take some of the parts in for teardown, but my gut tells me someone tampered with the plane's engine."

"What—" her voice cracked "—are you saying?"

"I'm still investigating, but I'm afraid your brother's plane may have been sabotaged."

All the blood rushed from her head. She blinked back the white dots clouding her vision. Eli's solid hand on the small of her back grounded her. "Someone killed my brother?" she muttered, flattening her hand against her stomach. Her worst fear was realized.

"I'm real sorry about your loss." Tim gestured with the clipboard. "I'll finish this report and get back to you."

"Thanks." Tim strode toward the office.

The deep rumble of a small plane vibrated through the shell of the hangar. A sleek jet taxied to the outside of the hangar. A black limousine she hadn't noticed before sat on the Tarmac. "Who's that?" she shouted over the roar of the engine. The hot air swept her hair back from her face.

Eli tented his hand over his eyes. He seemed to tense as the stairs on the plane popped out and a man appeared at the door. The man seemed to regard them for a moment before nodding in their direction. A second man followed him down the stairs.

Anna was surprised to see Tom Hanson step out of the driver's side of the limousine and walk around to open the back door, allowing Mr. Christopher, Tiffany and Chase's father, to step out. She saw a hint of long blond hair inside the limo. *Mrs. Christopher.*

"Maybe coming here wasn't such a good idea." Anna twisted her fingers, trying to tamp down her nervous energy.

"We're fine. Chase Christopher must be coming home to see his sister."

"Who's the other man with him?" Anna whispered.

"Bradley Blakely, the sheriff's son. He works with Chase. They went to college together." He ran his hand down Anna's arm. "They were all fraternity brothers."

Chase took his father's outstretched hand. His father gave him a hearty clap on the back. The men talked briefly before Mr. Christopher and Bradley climbed into the limo. Chase strolled over to Eli and Anna.

"To what does Apple Creek owe the visit of Special Agent Eli Miller?" Chase cocked an eyebrow. "I thought you left your backwoods way of life for the big city."

Eli tipped his head toward the wreckage. "The plane crash." He seemed to let his words sink in. "I hear your sister is doing better."

Anna couldn't make out Chase's eyes through the dark lenses of his sunglasses. "Yes, she is. Thank goodness." His brow furrowed over the top of the frames. "So, I imagine you'll be leaving soon."

Anna wrapped her hand around Eli's elbow. His muscles tensed, but he didn't say anything.

Chase seemed to be looking in her direction, but she couldn't be sure. "You must be Anna Quinn." She assumed he had seen her on the news. "Sorry about your brother. If there's anything the Christopher family can do, let me know. We were fraternity brothers. Fraternity brothers always take care of their own."

Anna narrowed her gaze at him. "Thank you." She hesitated a fraction. "I understand you talked to my brother recently."

Chase seemed to jerk his head back ever so slightly.

"What did you talk about? Did he tell you why he returned to Apple Creek?" Anna hated the desperation in her voice.

Chase plowed a hand through his thick hair. "Wasn't

he photographing the Amish for a coffee-table book?" He shrugged. "My job has me traveling like crazy. We really didn't have a chance to catch up. I mean, nothing more than a quick conversation. I understand he and my sister were friendly." He bowed his head slightly. "Thank goodness she wasn't killed. She has a long recovery in front of her."

"Chase—" Mrs. Christopher strode toward them, her high heels clacking on the cement floor of the hangar "—your sister is expecting us."

Chase gave them a cool smile. "My family is waiting." He started to walk away, then he turned back around. "Do you plan to have a service for Daniel? I'd like to attend."

"I haven't had a chance to plan it. I still have to take care of my brother's things."

Mrs. Christopher wrapped her hand possessively around her son's arm. "I would appreciate it if you cleared out your brother's things soon." She narrowed her gaze. "I think it would be cathartic if you boxed everything up and donated it all to charity. You need to move on with your life." She patted her son's arm. "I could have Tom take care of it. This really must be horrible for you." Her unusually smooth forehead failed to convey the right touch of sympathy. "Why delay the inevitable?"

"No, thank you. I'd like to go through my brother's things myself."

"Tom really wouldn't mind. Just say the word." She glanced up at her son. "Come on."

"Let me know when the service is." Chase gave her a thin-lipped smile.

Anna watched them climb into the vehicle. The limo made a U-turn and the back window slid down. Something in Mrs. Christopher's blank expression made icy fear course through her veins.

* * *

Eli took Anna's hand as she stepped over the trampled cornstalks at the site of the crash. They had struck out at the hangar and with the second search of Daniel's apartment. No flash drive. No camera. *Nothing.* Anna couldn't shake the dread that had descended on her after their visit to her brother's crumpled plane.

Squaring her shoulders, Anna steeled herself for the site in front of her—the place where her brother's plane crashed. Unable to tear her eyes away from the scorched earth, she wondered what her brother's last thoughts were. Closing her eyes, she covered her mouth to stifle a sob.

Anna bowed her head and offered a quick prayer that her brother no longer suffered. That he was at peace. That she and Eli would find peace. That they both would find the answers they needed. She stole a glance at Eli as he walked slowly, flashlight in hand, searching the charred earth. Determination fueling her, she stepped forward, the stalks crunching under her feet.

The sun hung low in the sky. Something about the shadowy fields made the hairs on her arms stand up, and it had nothing to do with the accident. Or maybe it had everything to do with it. All around her, the land seemed to stretch forever, yet the stalks of corn closed in on her.

Anna joined Eli in crisscrossing the area. The beams of the flashlights were aimed at the ground. Eli reasoned that the light would bounce off the metal of a flash drive or camera, making it easier to find now versus in the bright sunshine.

Anna directed her flashlight at the damp soil. "You think my brother found something and someone wanted him dead?"

"I'm afraid so." Eli bowed his head and swatted at his neck. "And based on recent events, I think they're still looking for it." Something in his tone made her look up. He grabbed her forearm, his eyebrows drawing together. "I don't want you out of my sight."

His possessive touch sent a flush of tingles racing across her flesh. Apparently sensing her unease, he let go and the lines around his eyes softened. "I don't want anything to happen to you."

Averting her gaze, Anna made a show of slapping at a mosquito on her arm. She quickly changed the subject. "Let's search the area before it gets any later."

The bent cornstalks crunched under Anna's tennis shoes. Her eyes tracked the beam of the flashlight. Eli trudged forward and looped back the other way, both of their heads bowed. After about thirty minutes of crisscrossing the site and a little farther beyond, Anna plopped down, completely oblivious to the damp earth seeping through her pants. She hugged her legs to her chest and watched Eli continue the fruitless search. He had a look of determination. A look of a man possessed.

Hopelessness overwhelmed her. "We're not going to find anything, are we?" She held up her palms. "It could be anywhere."

Eli sighed heavily. "It's not looking good."

Anna scratched her forehead. "We don't know if the photos are of any value. My brother didn't give me much to go on in the email."

Eli plopped down next to her, bumping her shoulder. "I'm not giving up on this."

Anna rested her elbows on her knees. "I know. We have to find the truth."

A crunching sound came from behind them. Eli scrambled to his feet and shone a flashlight in the direction of the noise. A young man, his eyes shadowed by a wide-brimmed hat, approached. He seemed to be looking past her to Eli.

No, he was staring at an empty space. *The crash site.* His haunted look unnerved her. It took her a minute to recognize Samuel, Eli's fifteen-year-old brother.

"Hi, Samuel." Eli lowered the beam of his flashlight, sending the features of his brother's face into darker shadows. He strode over and clapped his younger brother on the shoulder. "How's it going?"

"Do you think he went to heaven?" Samuel's question startled Anna.

"He is at peace," Eli said, his tone convincing.

Closing her eyes, Anna prayed silently. *Please let him be at peace.*

"I better go before *Dat* comes looking for me. I have chores."

"Wait," Eli called to his brother. His kindness toward his little brother reminded her of her own brother. Pressing her fist to her lips, she felt hollow inside. "Did you see the plane crash? You're usually outside doing chores...."

Anxiety spurred her to her feet. She swiped at her damp jeans, her eyes intently focused on Samuel. His brown eyes grew wide. Anna couldn't help but wonder if this was what Eli looked like when he was growing up in the Amish community.

Samuel tugged on the brim of his hat, shading his eyes. "I was walking from the barn when I heard a loud noise." The boy looked up and gestured with his hands, like wings of a plane. "I saw a plane close. Closer than I've seen the other planes when they use the Apple Creek Airpark." He had a faraway look in his eyes. "It made a horrible sputtering sound. The wings clipped a few trees before it hit...." His gaze dropped to the scorched earth. "I ran over in this direction."

Anna's heart squeezed. Hearing about her brother's last

minutes of life tore at her heart. The terror he must have experienced.

"Did you tell anyone what you saw?" Eli asked.

"No. *Dat* told us not to talk to the English coming to gawk at another man's misfortune."

Eli leaned over to meet the boy eye-to-eye. "There's nothing to be afraid of. Did you tell *Dat?*"

"No." Samuel stared in the direction of the crushed stalks as if reliving the moment.

"Did you approach the plane?" Anna's pulse thudded in her ears.

"He…he—" Samuel pushed his hat up and scratched his forehead "—he was hanging upside down." His eyes grew red. "All I could think about is how the Amish aren't supposed to fly."

"You saw him?" Anna nearly crumbled to her knees. She feared she wouldn't hear his response over the whooshing in her ears.

"I need to go. *Dat* will be looking for me." The teen turned and ran off, not answering her question.

Anna watched him disappear through the cornstalks. "Do you think my brother suffered?"

"It happened so fast."

"Your brother seems troubled. I think he's not telling us everything." As a counselor, she had experience with kids in crisis.

"It had to be hard to witness an accident like that."

"But why didn't he speak up sooner?" She tried to soften the edge in her voice. "He saw the crash. Maybe there's more he's not telling us. He said he saw my brother." Why did this give her hope? Her brother was dead. Nothing changed that.

"You don't understand. The Amish are reluctant to get involved in what they consider English problems. I'll talk

to him later. He might be reluctant to talk in front of you."
Eli closed the distance between them and took her hand.
"He's entering a tough stage in his life. My parents will be
encouraging him to get baptized. But as a young man, he'll
be tempted to explore the outside world."

Anna's mouth bowed into a small smile. "I suppose that's
why they don't like you hanging around. You're an example
of the outside world."

Something akin to hurt descended into his eyes. "I'm
going to search the area one more time."

Anna lifted her face to the sky. The sun had fully set
and a million stars dotted the night sky, making her feel
small. The crunch of Eli's footsteps on the dried cornstalks
floated back to her. She was glad she wasn't alone.

Eli adjusted the knob on the lamp and the light grew
brighter. He sat on the edge of the bed, exhausted but not
quite ready for sleep. He had hoped to talk with Samuel
this evening but couldn't find him. He supposed his little
brother was out in the barn tending to Red. He'd give him
more time before he forced him to talk about the crash.
They'd catch up at some point because they were sharing
the same sleeping quarters.

Scrubbing a hand across his face, he yawned. At home,
he would have flopped down on the couch and channel
surfed until his mind numbed into oblivion and sleep stole
over him, even if temporarily. Despite having grown up in
an Amish home, he had quickly grown accustomed to
modern conveniences. And mind-deadening technology.

With nothing but silence to keep him company, his
thoughts drifted. Eli had been a dutiful son his entire childhood. The day Mary disappeared, he had prayed and prayed
for her safe return. Two days later, when Mary's bed was
still empty, he decided God was not a merciful God. Right

then and there he abandoned his plain ways. The only time he found peace over the years was when he was absorbed in a case, helping some victim or their family find closure. The only way he would find true peace would be when he solved Mary's case.

His father cleared his throat. Eli snapped his attention toward the door. "Will you take a walk with me, Eli?" Abram asked.

Eli followed his father through the kitchen, grabbing his coat from the hook on the way out. The cloudless night afforded him a view of a million stars. In the city, light pollution drowned out the crisp view of the stars. The stillness here was peaceful as long as he didn't let his thoughts get in the way.

Abram walked toward the barn and Eli followed, knowing his father would tell him what was on his mind when he was ready. He slowed by the barn door and turned to face his son. "The plane has been cleared away from our fields."

"Yes, they didn't waste any time." A dark line furrowed his father's brow. "I thought that would make you happy. You'll be able to finish harvesting the corn for feed."

"Nothing about this situation makes me happy."

Eli bit his lip, knowing better than to argue with his father. "Are you anxious for me to go?"

"Son, we never wanted you to leave in the first place. *You* made your choice."

"I did. And I made the decision before I was baptized." There was no reason for his family to shun him. That was reserved for baptized members who turned their backs on the Ordnung, the set of Amish rules that governed their community. By shunning wayward members, the Amish hoped they'd see the error of their ways. Yet returning home for Eli had never been the same. He'd never be fully welcomed. He could see disappointment in his father's eyes and hurt in his mother's. And he was never encouraged to stay long. He didn't want to get his parents in trouble with the bishop. The Amish set themselves apart for a reason. There were too many distractions and temptations in the outside world.

"I know." His father angled his head so the brim of his hat shadowed his eyes. "We miss you, son, but we have to be careful. Your mother heard talk in town. The bishop thinks we are too tolerant of your visits." Abram's voice grew quiet. "And ever since your arrival, Samuel seems agitated. He admires you and I fear he's curious about your way of life."

Abram ran a hand down his beard. "Samuel has been venturing into town. I'm not sure who he is visiting. He seems to have taken a liking to Isaac, but I fear Samuel might want to explore the world like Isaac did."

"I will see what I can find out."

"Thank you." Abram squared his shoulders. "And I think for your own peace of mind, it's time for you to let Mary go. Until then, you'll never find peace."

Eli tried to relax his clenched jaw. "I can never let her go. I have to find answers."

"What if those answers lead to Daniel Quinn? Justice is not for this world anymore. Can you live with hurting Anna? She is blameless in all this."

"I have to find the truth. It was my fault Mary disappeared. I should have never let her out of my sight."

"It's not your fault." His father's voice was stern.

Eli's throat closed around his grief.

"We have forgiven whoever took our Mary. We don't want anyone else to be hurt."

Eli's grief shifted into anger. "No one has been arrested." He had grown tired of having this argument with his father.

"It doesn't matter. We have forgiven him. I have faith

Mary has found peace. And we are at peace with our forgiveness."

But the ever-present pain he always saw in his mother's eyes revealed something perhaps his father was unwilling to accept. His mother may have proclaimed her forgiveness, but her eyes radiated the pain of a mother who has lost a child.

"You cannot come into our home and continue this hunt. It serves no purpose."

"Someone has to pay."

"Retribution is not our way."

"Father, didn't you love your Mary?"

Abram took a moment before speaking, his eyes heavily shadowed, but Eli noticed his lips trembled. "A father loves his children."

"Then how can you forgive so easily?" *Especially when I have not been able to forgive myself.*

NINE

Anna splashed cold water on her face, then patted it dry with a towel. The linens smelled of fresh air, unlike any scented detergent. She was grateful Eli's family allowed indoor plumbing because she had learned that not all Amish communities did. She yanked the clip from her hair, letting it cascade down her shoulders. Leaning close to the mirror, she pressed on the flesh under her eyes. The dim light from the oil lamp in the bathroom did nothing to help her appearance, yet it accurately reflected how she felt. Tired, drained, exhausted. The weight of the world on her shoulders.

With her small overnight bag in hand, she tiptoed down the hallway to her room, hoping she wouldn't run into anyone. As she neared the top of the stairs, she heard voices floating up from the sitting room. Curious, she wanted to go see who it was but felt underdressed in her T-shirt and cotton pajama pants. She lingered at the top of the stairs.

"Sorry to stop by so late. I only now heard about the horrible accident," a woman said, her voice shaky, older perhaps.

"Oh, Sara, you could have waited till morning. How is your daughter?"

The woman sighed. "The trip seems longer each time I take it. I so wish she lived closer. But her husband was determined to settle nearer his parents."

Anna slipped to her bedroom and dropped the toiletries on the dresser. She grabbed a sweatshirt out of her suitcase and jammed her arms into it. Smoothing a hand over her hair, she descended the stairs. She was about to make her presence known when she heard Mariam speak.

"God tells us to lay our worries in his hands, but I am filled with concern for my son Samuel." A mix of anxiety and shame laced Mariam's voice.

Anna thought about Eli's younger brother, the stress on his face when they saw him in the field this afternoon.

"He's always been quiet. Too quiet. I fear he's never gotten over losing his twin." Her delicate tone belied the gravity of her words.

"Poor Mary." The older woman tsk-tsked.

"My faith in God has sustained me." Mariam's voice was barely a whisper. "My faith is strong, but so is my motherly instinct. We are losing him."

"I know how hard it was for you when Eli left." The older woman's voice grew quiet. "I hear he's staying here."

"Oh, only for a day or two. He's here because of the crash." Anna's heart squeezed at the defensiveness in Mariam's voice.

"Some of the neighbors are talking."

"Let them talk," Mariam said in what Anna suspected was a rare display of defiance. "God will never forgive me for not trusting in His plan, but I've already lost two children. I can't lose a third. Abram doesn't want to discuss it. I think he fears we are inviting trouble."

Anna pulled her sleeves down over her hands and stifled a shudder. Clearing her voice, she stepped into the entryway of the sitting room. "I'm sorry to interrupt."

Mariam jumped to her feet. "I didn't realize you were awake." She held out her palm to the older woman. "This is my aunt Sara."

Anna nodded. "Hello." Embarrassment heated her cheeks. "I don't mean to pry, but why do you think you will lose Samuel?"

Mariam seemed to regard the older woman for a moment. Sara lowered her gaze and folded her hands in her lap. "He is approaching Rumspringa." Anna gave her a confused look, so Mariam explained. "His running around time. He'll have a chance to explore the outside world, relax the rules a bit, before he commits to the Amish way. Before he is baptized. He so reminds me of Eli. I fear he might look to the outside world to search for something he thinks he's missing here."

Mariam fidgeted with the fabric of her apron. She looked up with steely resolve. "He loves his brother so. Any words from him may be encouragement to leave the Amish."

"I don't think Eli would encourage him to leave his home."

Mariam lifted her palms. "I have said too much."

Sara stood and Mariam followed suit.

"Nice to meet you, Sara."

Sara nodded, then she turned to her niece. "You should talk to Abram about your worries."

"You're right." Mariam bowed. "I will talk to him when he gets in." She twisted her hands. "He and Samuel have been spending a lot of time in the barn with Red. Poor creature."

A stiff breeze blew in through the open window. Anna tucked a strand of hair behind her ear. The chirp of crickets filled the air.

Sara paused in front of Anna and gave her a pointed glare. "English life can be hard."

Anna crossed her arms, then let them fall to her side. "I'm sure everyone has their moments."

"My husband told me about your family."

"Sara—" Mariam's tone held an urgent quality "—Anna's brother died in the plane crash."

"I am sorry for that. But do you think it's wise she stay here?"

Anna's cheeks burned hot. "What do you mean? It's only temporary. Surely no one will have issue with that."

"The sheriff stopped my husband when he was in town today." She smoothed her hands down her skirt. "He thought we should know who was staying in our community."

"What did the sheriff tell you?" Anna bit her cheek, realizing her initial distaste for the sheriff was well founded.

"He told us about your poor mother...." No doubt, the sheriff had told her how her father killed her mother. How her brother was suspected in hurting Mary.

Grateful for the dim lighting, Anna tipped her head back to hold off the tears blurring her vision. "I will move to a motel first thing in the morning." The thought of staying at her brother's apartment after someone broke into it, unnerved her. "The last thing I want to do is cause your family any more trouble."

"You don't have to leave." Mariam said, her voice barely a whisper. "I am sorry I made you feel like you had to leave. Considering the circumstances—" Mariam met her aunt Sara's perplexed gaze "—I'm sure no one in the community would fault us for welcoming the English into our home during their time of need."

Sara pursed her lips. "It's late. I must be going." Sara slipped out the door. By the starlight Anna could see the older woman climb up into a buggy. A man flicked his wrists and the jangle of the harness and the crunching of the wheels on the gravel competed with the calls of the night critters.

Mariam sighed and lowered herself into the rocker, seemingly defeated. It was obvious she didn't have a stomach for conflict. "Abram and I already knew your brother was under investigation regarding our sweet Mary before my aunt arrived. We didn't know, however, about your parents. I'm sorry. I have been too wrapped up in my own worries." Mariam's eyes brightened. "None of this affects our feelings for you. We forgive whoever took our Mary."

Anger flashed below the surface. "I don't need your forgiveness, Mrs. Miller."

Mariam bowed her head. "I didn't mean to offend you." She got up, crossed over to the window and slid it shut, cutting off the cacophony of night critters. Without the cool evening breeze, the walls pushed in.

Anna turned to Mariam, who was standing motionless. "I'm sorry to have caused your family so much turmoil. I will be sure to leave in the morning." She didn't want to stay where they'd be looking at her, pitying her. She had had enough of that as a teenager—the whispers in the hallway in high school, the taunts, the pointing and staring. Kids were cruel.

Yet her heart went out to Mariam and her family. She was a school counselor, so maybe she'd be able to help Samuel with his feelings of loss. She couldn't turn away from a lost soul. "Perhaps I could talk to Samuel. I work with teenagers every day. Maybe I can help him come to terms with his feelings."

Shaking her head, Mariam wrung her hands. "That won't be necessary."

"What won't be necessary?" Abram stood in the doorway. His face was hidden in shadow, but the angry edge to his question left no room for interpretation.

Anna started to speak, but Mariam interrupted, her voice quiet in submission to her husband's authority. "Anna and I were having a chat. She has a lot on her mind since her brother's accident."

"Is everything okay?" Eli strolled up next to his father.

Mariam squared her shoulders and hiked her chin. "Everything's fine. I must go check on Katie Mae." She brushed past her husband.

Abram watched his wife stride out of the sitting room without a word. His eyes then landed on Anna. "We don't want our children to have undue influence from outsiders. You'd be wise to remember that."

Anna shoved her feet into her tennis shoes and ran outside. The wooden door slammed against the door frame, sending her nerves into overdrive. The tragedy from her past had caught up with her. Even out here on this Amish farm. A world away. She filled her lungs with the sweet country night air. Streaks of billowy clouds floated across the moon. The earthy smell reached her nose. Taking in the beautiful display calmed her rioting emotions, even if only a fraction.

She knew she couldn't go back inside just yet. The walls would surely close in on her. As she strolled toward the barn, the silhouette of a young Amish man and his dog came into view. She glanced back toward the house. No one would be the wiser if she happened to talk to Samuel. Maybe she could help. She pulled the sleeves of her sweatshirt down over her hands and strode faster toward the barn as the young man disappeared inside. Her tennis shoes kicked up the occasional pebble.

The red barn stood adjacent to the rows and rows of corn. The barn door yawned open. She peered inside, but it was heavily cloaked in shadows. "Samuel." Her call was met with silence and her muscles tensed. "Samuel, it's Anna. I want to talk."

"About what?" Samuel stepped into the opening, a serious look on his face. Ice formed in her veins.

"Your mother is worried about you."

Samuel's brow furrowed. "It is not our place to worry. We must trust God's plan." His words held a trace of irony. Had he been eavesdropping on her conversation with his mother through the open window? She didn't accuse him for fear of chasing him away.

Anna dug deep. "Maybe God brought me here so you'd have someone to talk to." Samuel hitched an eyebrow in obvious skepticism. "It's okay to talk about something when it's bothering you."

"I know what your brother did." His words grew hard, his tone that of someone much older than his fifteen years.

"My brother didn't hurt your sister if that's what you're thinking." It took a lot of control to hold her voice steady.

"The sheriff thinks he did." He tugged on the brim of his hat. "Isaac thinks he did." His words held a challenge. "And Eli has been investigating him."

Anna flinched. His words cut her to the core. "I know you're hurting, but I know my brother. He would have never hurt a child." She rubbed the sleeves of her sweatshirt. "When I was twelve, my parents both died." She didn't bother explaining the gory truth. "My brother was all I had. He took care of me. He wasn't perfect, but he was good at heart. And that's what counts."

Samuel stood frozen in place, glaring at her while Red disappeared deeper into the barn.

"He even took me to church." Guilt nagged at her conscience. "But I'm not out here to talk about my brother. I want to talk about you."

A rustling came from the dark confines of the barn. Unfamiliar with the agricultural life, Anna couldn't decipher it, but it seemed to pique Samuel's interest. "Is everything okay?"

"I'm worried about Red. She's getting old."

"I never had a pet. Always wanted one, though." She searched his face to see if she was reaching him. Samuel scratched his head, seemingly bored.

"Your mom is concerned you will leave home like Eli did." Samuel jerked his head back, as if the thought surprised him. "If you heard the stories around town about my parents, you might think that beyond this farm is a big bad scary world." Anna held up her palms and looked around. "A lot of English might agree. But I can't tell you that. You have to make your own decision. If things are bothering you in here—" she pointed to her heart "—you won't be able to automatically fix them out there." She pointed toward the country road. "You have to work on what's inside first."

She couldn't make out Samuel's eyes shadowed by the brim of his hat. "I can't believe my parents are allowing you to stay in our home. Your brother ruined everything." His voice cracked.

Anna's breath hitched. "I plan to find a motel in the morning."

"It would be best if you left Apple Creek all together."

"Who told you I should leave Apple Creek?"

"Isaac." Rounding his shoulders, Samuel turned on his heel and disappeared into the darkened barn.

"Samuel…Samuel, come back here." A loud thud vibrated from deep in the barn. Concern blossomed in her chest.

"Samuel?" No answer. Goose bumps blanketed her skin.

The hay crunched under her feet as she stepped into the barn. Slivers of moonlight leaked in through the wood slats. She recognized the outline of a tractor and another door opening toward the fields.

"Samuel?" She found herself whispering. The loft creaked. An uneasy sense of hyperawareness coursed through her. The scent of dry hay filled her nostrils. A sprinkling of something rained down on her shoulders. "Samuel, are you up there? Please, let's talk." A dark shadow filled her field of vision. Something slammed into her head, driving her to the ground. Her head hit the hard-packed earth and her final awareness was filled with icy panic for Samuel's well-being.

TEN

We don't want our children to have undue influence from outsiders. Abram's words rang in Eli's ears as he watched Anna storm past him and out the back door. His father had been speaking to Anna, but the full implication of his message landed squarely on Eli's shoulder. *He* was the outsider. He was the one his father feared would have undue influence on his children. He watched his father hang his hat on the hook by the door. Intuitively, he already knew this, but to hear it spoken with such clarity was like a knife to the heart.

Had Eli been deluding himself? Did he really believe that when he found Mary or her kidnapper he'd be welcomed home the hero? *No,* he'd forever be the outsider. The Amish way was to forgive.

But not their own.

As long as he refused to come back into the fold, he'd never be forgiven. They saw his need for justice as a form of revenge. In their eyes, revenge only got in the way of redemption. Because he turned away from the church, his parents feared for his soul. Now they feared for their other children. He ran a hand across his whiskered jaw.

His father put his hand on the banister at the bottom of the stairs. "Good night."

"I must find out what happened to Mary. You know that. It's something I have to do."

Abram bowed his head, as if gathering his thoughts. "You were raised to do what is right for the common good. I did not raise you to pursue personal goals. You must be humble. Accept God's will."

Eli curled his fingers into fists. God's will had not dictated his sister's disappearance. It had been the evil hand of man. He bit back a retort. He knew he'd get nowhere. He had been living in the outside world for over ten years now. He didn't know how to rein in the emotions that sliced through him. "This is hardly a personal goal. I need to know what happened to Mary. I cannot rest until justice is served. For Mary's sake."

Abram climbed one stair and glanced over his shoulder. "Do you think you will be happy then?"

Eli rubbed a hand across the back of his neck. He doubted he'd ever be happy. Nothing would bring back his little sister. He stared after his father as he climbed the stairs.

Feeling caged, Eli strode onto the back porch, holding the door so it wouldn't slam in its frame. Having seen Anna go out the back door, he had expected to find her on the back porch. Mild concern whispered across his brain. He started to cross the yard when he heard barking coming from the barn.

When he reached the barn, Red was barking wildly. Eli's heart stopped when he saw Anna's thin frame sprawled out on the barn floor.

"Anna." He ran the short distance and dropped down beside her. "Anna." He pushed away the hay bale resting on her shoulder. "Can you hear me?" He pressed his fingers to her delicate throat. When he found her pulse, he released the breath he hadn't realized he'd been holding.

He slipped one arm under her legs, the other under her arms and picked her up. She was light, delicate. Something inside him stirred. Why did he feel so protective of her? *Forever the champion of the underdog?* He smelled the coconut scent of her shampoo. He felt the steady up and down of her chest as he carried her. He turned to bring her into the house when a shadow appeared in the doorway. He froze for a fraction before he realized it was his younger brother.

"What are you doing here? Did you see what happened?" Eli asked, a sharp edge to his tone.

Samuel stood stock-still, his features unreadable in the dark shadows. "Is she dead?"

"No." Losing patience, Eli pushed past him. "Let me get her into the house."

Eli rushed with her toward the house. Tendrils of awareness whispered across the back of his neck. He turned around on the porch and stared into the darkness, certain someone was staring back.

Unfamiliar voices stirred Anna from a restless sleep. No, wait, she didn't remember going to bed. The events of last night emerged as if from a slowly lifting fog. *The barn...?* She forced her eyes open. A pounding thudded under her skull with the effort. Blinking against the light, she recognized Eli's concerned face.

"Hey there." A small smile turned up the corners of his mouth. The edge of the bed dipped where he sat. "You had us all scared." He ran his warm finger across her forehead.

Pain seared across her brain as she moved her gaze around the room. Mariam and Abram stood in the far corner and young Samuel hung back by the door. "What happened?" she asked through her parched lips.

Eli tucked a strand of hair behind her ear. "I was hoping you could tell us."

Closing her eyes, she thought back to the last few moments she remembered. "Something fell on me. I think it was a hay bale from the loft." She leaned up on her elbow and a sharp pain shot up her neck.

Eli adjusted the pillows under her head. "Relax. We need to take you to the hospital. Make sure nothing is broken. See if you have a concussion."

With her eyes closed, Anna held up her hand. The last place she wanted to go was the hospital. "Let me rest a few minutes. I think I'm fine."

"Did you see anyone?" Eli asked. Anna realized for the first time that he was holding her hand and rubbing the pad of his thumb gently across the back of her hand. Something warm coiled around her heart. No, he was simply offering comfort because that's the kind of man he was. Shame she met the right man at the wrong time.

"I…" She opened her eyes and strained to see Samuel's expression as he stood in the doorway. His mouth was drawn into a grimace. She had to earn his trust. Her eyes moved to Abram. A pain scratched across her brain with the sudden movement. Maybe she did have a concussion. She squinted. Eli's father seemed to be studying his youngest son. She could only imagine the intense pressure this boy felt as he moved into adulthood with the expectation that he be baptized. Or risk becoming an outsider.

"No," she lied, "I didn't see anyone. I wandered into the barn and before I knew what happened, something fell on me." Her eyes met Eli's. "Is it unusual for things to fall off the barn loft?"

It was Abram who spoke up, his voice tight. "We may be plain people, but we take pride in our work. We do not stack things such that they might fall and injure someone."

Anna ran a hand across her forehead. "I didn't mean to

imply…" She stopped talking. Each word pinged her aching brain.

"We will let you rest." Mariam led Abram and Samuel from the room. Eli hung back, still sitting on the edge of the bed, holding her hand.

"You spoke to Samuel before you were injured," Eli whispered, not bothering to frame it as a question.

Anna nodded, immediately regretting the movement. "Your father wouldn't have approved. I need to gain Samuel's trust to help him. He seems angry." She rubbed her temple. "Or maybe sad. He hasn't dealt with the loss of his twin sister." Her chest grew heavy with the realization. "And thanks to the town gossips, he thinks I'm the sister of the devil himself."

Flashlight in hand, Eli climbed the wooden ladder to the barn loft. The smell of hay melted the years away. When he was a kid, he'd climb up here to play hooky from his chores—only long enough to read a few pages, not long enough to get scolded by his father. It seemed impossible the memories belonged to him. A young Amish boy. A lifetime ago. He shoved aside the past and focused on the task at hand.

The shaft of light from his flashlight illuminated the old wood beams and hay bales. No sign of anything precariously close to the edge. Stepping farther onto the loft, he tested his weight on the beams. A lone hay bale sat near the back along the wall. As he approached, his flashlight lit on a small pile of cigarettes stubbed out on a flat rock. He ran his hand over the back of his neck, wondering if Samuel had taken to smoking, a habit not quite banned by the Amish but certainly frowned upon. The elders looked the other way, praying the young and foolish would give up the vice once they were baptized. He'd have to talk to his little brother, not that he'd listen to him.

They all had bigger issues right now.

Had Samuel accidentally knocked a hay bale over the edge and now was afraid to speak up? Afraid he'd be scolded for smoking or for hurting Anna?

He was about to turn on his heel when a crumpled piece of paper among the loose strands of hay caught his eye. He picked it up and flattened it on his thigh. It was a page torn from a yearbook or maybe downloaded from a website. It only took him a second before he saw it—a portrait of Miss Quinn, School Counselor. His heart kicked up a notch. He directed his flashlight around the space, looking for something, but he wasn't sure what. Crouching, he tried to get at the same level as the smoker would be using the rock as an ashtray.

That's when he saw it. A knot in the wood. He peered through the hole it formed. From this position, he had a clear view of his parents' home and the window of Anna's bedroom. His gut tightened. This hadn't been an accident. Someone was determined to run Anna out of town, or worse. If not for dumb luck—or perhaps the grace of God—they may have succeeded tonight.

Daniel's concerned face flashed in his mind. "Watch out for my sister," he had warned the week before he died. Had someone threatened to hurt Anna if Daniel didn't stop whatever he was doing? But why try to hurt Anna now that Daniel was dead? Maybe they were concerned Anna wouldn't rest until she uncovered whatever her brother had.

Tucking the paper into his back pocket, he climbed down from the loft. He did a quick canvass of the barn and nearby property before making his way across the yard to the farmhouse. He found Anna sitting up in bed, her hand on her forehead and her face pale.

"Are you okay?" He frowned. Without waiting for an answer, he slipped his arm around her waist. "Come on, I'm taking you to the emergency room. You might have a concussion." Grimacing, Anna eased her legs out of bed and didn't argue with him.

Definitely not a good sign.

Eli tapped on the glass of the triage station in the emergency room that served the rural community. It was a far cry from the hustle and bustle of a city E.R. All the same, the composed nurse looked up at him and rolled her eyes. The nurse had obviously dealt with anxious loved ones hundreds of times. "Sir, you'll have to wait your turn. We had a car accident come in." The nurse gave him a pointed glare, then went back to the computer screen in front of her.

He sat down next to Anna in the orange plastic chairs arranged in a narrow U facing a television mounted on the wall. "I'm sorry. You holding up okay?"

"My stomach seems to have settled, but I have one horrendous headache." She squinted up at him before closing her eyes. He flicked his gaze to the harsh glare of the fluorescent lighting.

Eli glanced at the triage station but forced himself to sit tight. He was used to taking control, having his way. But even he couldn't justify pushing Anna ahead of a car accident victim. Glancing down, he noticed her trembling hands. Without asking for permission, he reached over, took her hand and pulled her toward him. He slipped his arm around her shoulders and let her rest her head on his chest. It felt right. But nothing good could come from falling for this woman. He had given up everything to find Mary and he didn't plan on stopping now. And if her brother was involved, their relationship would be doomed from the start. *How could two people ever get past that?*

He smoothed a hand down her hair, unable to resist the silky feel of it. For now, he'd have to settle for pretending.

"Well, well, well…" A familiar, yet smug, voice sounded from behind him. Eli turned to find the sheriff standing there, his lips twisted into a sardonic grin.

Eli gently shifted Anna out of his embrace and stood to face the sheriff. He crossed his arms. Why did it always feel like a turf war with this man?

"Are you here because of the car accident?" Eli asked.

"Not my jurisdiction."

Cocking an eyebrow, he waited for the sheriff to continue. "I'm here on a courtesy call," he finally said.

"Courtesy call?" The first twinges of escalating anger coursed through his veins. Was the sheriff following him?

"The Christophers called me. They would like to clear out Daniel's apartment." The sheriff leaned around Eli to get a look at Anna. Resting her elbow on the back of the chair, she supported her head in her hand.

"How did you know we were here?" Eli asked.

"Stopped by your parents' farm." The sheriff jerked his chin toward Anna. "What happened?"

"She bumped her head. I want to get her checked out. See if she has a concussion." Eli didn't want to clue the sheriff in on what he found in the loft, not yet anyway. He had come too far to lose control now. Ten years ago when Mary went missing he had seen firsthand how protective of an investigation the sheriff had become. As if bringing in outside help was an affront to his manhood. Besides, in this small town, the sheriff was a little too close to the Christophers.

"Bumped her head?" The sheriff stepped around Eli and approached Anna. All of Eli's defense mechanisms kicked into high gear. He needed to protect her from this bully. That's what the sheriff was. On the day Mary disappeared, he had tried to bully Eli into saying things that weren't true. Tried to accuse him of racing his buggy. Losing control. Hurting Mary. Even now the thought of it nearly snapped his thin thread of control. He had been too young, too naive to stand up to the man back then. Not anymore.

"Anna fell and bumped her head. We're seeking medical help. End of story." He glared down at the sheriff. "We will clean out Daniel's apartment by the end of the month. You can let the Christophers know."

The sheriff grimaced. "I want to hear for myself how Anna bumped her head." The sheriff pushed back his shoulders and narrowed his gaze. "As you well know, your family's farm is in my jurisdiction." A threat laced his tone.

Eli and Anna's gazes met. She must have read something in his eyes because she said, "It was stupid really. I wanted to see the horses and when one of them backed up, I jumped out of the way and slammed my head on the stall door." She shrugged, but the light-hearted gesture came off as strained.

"Eli, maybe you can check with the nurse while I talk to Anna alone." Eli was more than familiar with domestic abuse protocol. To isolate the parties so the victim can request help. Why would the sheriff take that approach? He knew he and Anna had only met recently. Unless he was trying to isolate Anna to intimidate her. To coerce her into going back to Buffalo. For some reason, Anna seemed to be a thorn in the Christopher family's side and the sheriff was always quick to protect them. And his own son who was a close friend of Chase Christopher's.

"You heard the lady. She told you she injured herself in the barn. Let her be. She's in a lot of pain."

The sheriff seemed to regard them for a moment. "I understand Daniel's body is scheduled for cremation tomorrow. You plan on leaving soon?"

Anna rose to her feet. Pain etched her features from the effort. "Sheriff, I need to clean out my brother's apartment and take care of a few things first."

"It would be best if you cleared out of the Christopher's property as soon as possible."

Eli watched the sheriff leave the E.R. Anna placed her hand on his forearm. "Why didn't you tell the sheriff the truth about my accident?"

"I don't trust him. I don't know who he's talking to and I don't want it to affect the investigation." He patted her hand, then turned and led her back to her chair.

Anna sat down slowly, wincing with the motion. "What is the truth, Eli?"

Eli dug a piece of paper out of his jean's pocket and unfolded it. Anna stared at the crumpled paper. A crease cut her face diagonally, giving her a warped look. "That's my staff photo from the high school yearbook." She looked up to meet Eli's gaze, and apprehension filled her eyes. "Where did you find that?"

"In the barn loft." He reached out and captured her hand in his. "It seems someone was watching you from the loft. I don't think they had planned on hurting you in the barn, but they took the opportunity when you happened to be in there."

"But why?" Her mind swirled with the possibilities.

"Do you have any enemies in Buffalo?" Eli asked, brushing a strand of hair from her face. "It wouldn't take much for them to follow you here."

Splaying her delicate hands, she said, "I'm a school counselor. Sure, I have the occasional angry student, but nothing out of the ordinary." Her hands curled into fists as she met his gaze. "This has to do with my brother, right? He found something that might incriminate someone in Mary's disappearance. Now they want me to go home so I don't uncover whatever information he had. Then they can pin Mary's kidnapping on him. Case closed. Nice and neat."

Eli scrubbed a hand across his face. "You could be right. But it doesn't add up. Now that Daniel's gone, as long as these attacks continue, it only proves that someone else has something to lose if we find whatever it is Daniel had."

"Obviously, they're desperate enough to take the chance. If we never figure out what Daniel had uncovered, the truth could remain buried forever."

Eli nodded. "And if someone's desperate, they won't stop—"

"You think someone will kill me if I don't leave well enough alone?" Fear flashed in her hazel eyes.

"I won't let that happen."

ELEVEN

"Thanks." Anna accepted the water from Eli and ran her free hand across the smooth grain of the arms of the rocking chair. The ache in her head had died down to a dull roar now that they were back at the Miller's home. Yet another painful thought whispered across her brain. *Someone killed Daniel, and now they're out to get me.*

Eli leaned forward in his rocker, a concerned look in his deep brown eyes. "I'd feel better if I could watch you for a little bit before you go to bed." The doctor said she had a mild concussion.

"I don't think I could sleep if I tried."

Eli stared straight ahead as if deep in thought. She studied his strong profile. She had only known him a short time, but his mere presence calmed her nerves. Having witnessed firsthand the destruction her father—a police officer—rained down on her family, she had vowed she'd never fall for anyone in law enforcement. She believed the difficulties of the job had turned her father into an evil man. And because he was a police officer, her mother had nowhere to turn.

Maybe she had been wrong.

She sipped the cool water. Eli was different. Wasn't he? She witnessed his compassion, his gentleness, his love of family even though they considered him an outsider. Her father could be the sweetest guy, too. He was never as contrite as he was the day after he brutally beat his wife. Her gaze drifted to Eli's strong hands. She had never seen them raised in anger. Maybe he *was* different. Her heart ached. He had a family right here, but they kept him at arm's length. She had none.

"Is it tough to be back here?" Immediately heat blossomed in her cheeks. "I mean…you grew up in an Amish community. This was your home. It's obvious your mother loves you dearly." His father was harder to read, but she imagined he cared for his eldest son in his own way. "Have you ever regretted your decision to leave? Have you lost all faith?"

Eli shifted in his chair to face her, the smooth planes of his features void of emotion. "The day my little sister disappeared was the day I lost faith."

"Maybe you would find peace if you went back to your faith."

Half his mouth curved into a grin. "Do you really see me as returning to the Amish way of life?"

A laugh bubbled up from Anna's lips. Pain scraped against her brain. "Ouch." She rubbed her forehead gently. "I didn't necessarily mean for you to go back to being Amish. But haven't you ever considered joining another church? Maybe it would bring you some peace. I know it did after my mother was killed." Pain sliced her heart even after all these years.

Eli braced the arms of his chair. "I'll find peace when I arrest the evil person who took my sister."

"What if that never happens?" she whispered.

"I can't think that way."

Silence stretched between them. Anna let her thoughts drift. An ache throbbed behind her eyes. "The sheriff is eager for me to leave town."

"It sure seems that way. The Christopher family is putting the screws to him." A muscle twitched in Eli's jaw. "That's how things sometimes work in small towns."

Anna searched his face. "Maybe I should leave. Take my brother's remains and go home." Part of her wanted him to ask her to stay. Another part of her wanted life to go back to normal.

Eli's lips thinned into a straight line. He pushed to his feet and crossed to the window, pulling back the single panel covering it. The silence stretched for too long. Unease prickled the back of her neck. She needed answers as much as he did.

When he turned around, she struggled to read his eyes in the dim light. Time seemed to come to a screeching halt as the back of her throat ached. "It would be safer if you left."

His unequivocal answer slicked her palms with sweat. She ran them across her thighs, struggling to stay composed. "I'd hate to bring danger to your family. I'll check into the motel in town."

Eli sat down and leaned in close, running a knuckle across the back of her hand. "You should go back to Buffalo. Out of harm's way. I'll have someone keep an eye on you for a while. Till I know this mess has blown over."

She sat up straight and narrowed her gaze. "You still have doubts about my brother. If I leave, it will be easier for you to put a neat little bow on your investigation." She regretted her words even as they poured from her mouth. She lowered her voice. "I have to know the truth."

She started to stand and Eli reached out and caught her

hand, forcing her back down. His words came out even and soft, barely audible above the frantic pulsing in her ears. "I want the truth, too."

The anger drained out of her. Tears stung the backs of her eyes and she couldn't contain them this time. Tear after tear trailed down her face. Eli reached out and dragged the pad of his thumb across her cheek.

She gently pushed his hand away. "I can't stay here. I can't put your family at risk. But I can't go home yet."

Eli stared at her with a distant look in his eyes. "You need to get a good night's rest. How are you feeling?" He reached out a hand.

"I'll be fine." She accepted his hand and stood up. A wave of pain swept over her, but she stifled a grimace.

"We'll figure things out in the morning. Come on." He wrapped his arm around her waist and they turned to go upstairs. In the doorway, Samuel held a camera by a long strap.

"Where did you get that?" Eli brushed past Anna.

Samuel stretched out his arm, letting the camera dangle. Eli reached for it, but Samuel jerked away. "It's for Anna."

Taking the strap, Anna's heart raced. She turned the cool metal over in her hands. It looked expensive. Slowly she lifted her head to meet Samuel's expectant gaze.

"Your brother gave it to me." With his mussed hair and night clothes, Samuel seemed far younger than his fifteen years.

"I don't understand. Is this…?" With trembling fingers, she flicked the camera's on button but nothing happened.

"The morning of the accident…" Samuel's voice floated through a long tunnel. She stepped backward. The back of her legs hit the chair. She plopped down, not taking her eyes off the teenager. "I saw the accident. When I reached the plane, he was bleeding pretty badly from his head. I almost ran away. I wanted to get the neighbors. They have a phone. I wanted to call for help." He scratched his head, leaving thick, dark tufts of hair standing on end. "But the man was trying to tell me something. I couldn't make out the words. He tossed the camera toward me." Samuel pointed to it with a shaky finger.

"My brother was conscious after he crashed?" Disbelief edged her words.

Samuel nodded. "I was afraid. I didn't know what to do."

Eli placed his hand on his brother's shoulder. "It's okay. Tell us what happened."

"I don't want to get in trouble." Samuel studied the floor.

"Why would you get in trouble?" Eli leaned down to meet Samuel eye-to-eye.

"Isaac gave me a radio a few months ago and *Dat* found it. I promised him I wouldn't use any banned items."

"You understand this is different?"

Samuel stared blankly at him. "I knew it was wrong, yet I let my curiosity get the best of me. I wanted to see how the camera worked." He lowered his gaze. "I couldn't figure it out."

"Did my brother say anything?" Anna's face had grown ghostly white.

"He was moaning. I thought he said, 'Mary.'" He shrugged, a poor attempt at acting nonchalant.

"Mary? Are you sure?" Eli struggled to keep his tone even.

Samuel stared off in the distance. "That's all he said. *Mary.* I thought maybe the girl in the plane with him was named Mary, but when I learned later her name was Tiffany, I got scared because then I thought maybe he was talking about our Mary." He looked up with watery eyes.

"Why would he be talking about our sister?" His face crumpled in confusion.

Eli squeezed his brother's shoulder. "You did the right thing by giving us the camera."

"You won't tell *Dat* I had the camera, will you?" Samuel spoke in a whisper, his lower lip trembling.

Eli patted his brother's shoulder reassuringly. "No one needs to know you had this. The important thing is you came forward now." He narrowed his gaze. "Did you tell anyone about the camera?"

Samuel bowed his head and dragged his bare foot across the floor. "Well, I didn't exactly tell anyone. But I did ask Isaac if he thought having a picture taken was really going against the Bible. He asked me why I cared so much because it wasn't like I'd ever have one." He slowly lifted his head.

Samuel glanced at Anna, a look of contrition on his face. "I'm real sorry about running away from you. It's my fault you got hurt in the barn. You would have never been in the barn if I hadn't run through there."

"It wasn't your fault." She flicked her gaze momentarily to Eli. "You can't blame yourself."

Samuel fisted his hands at his side. "I can't deal with any more guilt."

"What are you talking about Samuel?" Eli asked.

Samuel looked at him with hesitant eyes. "The day Mary disappeared, I was teasing her. I pulled off her *kapp* and yanked her hair. She went with you because she wanted to get away from me." His shoulders rounded and he sobbed. "It's all my fault."

"No, that's not true." Eli grabbed both his brother's upper arms in a reassuring brace. "You were just a kid. You were only five years old."

Samuel's eyes grew wide. "But don't you understand?

If I hadn't been a pest, she would have been helping me dust off the benches for the worship service in the barn. She wouldn't have been with you in town. Because of me, my whole family was destroyed."

TWELVE

The next morning, Eli slipped behind the wheel of his SUV and glanced over at Anna. She cradled Daniel's camera in her lap as if it were a baby. He reached across the center console and patted her knee. "Once we get new batteries, we'll know what's on there."

Anna nodded. "I know. Do you think my brother gave the camera to Samuel because he didn't want someone to get ahold of it?" She traced a finger along the top of the camera and glanced out the window. "Do you think having this puts us in danger?"

"The thought crossed my mind. We'll have to keep it low key." Eli reached behind the seat and pulled out a small black canvas bag. "Put it in here."

Fidgeting with the zipper of the bag, Anna finally got it open and placed the camera gingerly inside. "If Daniel had photographic evidence, why do you think he didn't tell you?" He noted the apprehension in her voice.

Eli ran his hand across the top of the steering wheel. "I don't know. Maybe he was paranoid it would make him look guilty." A quiet groan left her lips. "Don't borrow trouble. Wait and see."

"You said the FBI was all over his fraternity, right? I bet

my brother had his suspicions. He came back to uncover the truth himself."

"Possibly." He tilted his head to try to get a read on her emotions. "But why not stick around in the first place? Why drop out and enlist in the army?"

She sighed, obviously exasperated. "Because you guys—" She seemed to catch herself. "The FBI was narrowing in on him because of his past. Who better to accuse than a guy who had once been under investigation for his parents' deaths? He chose to enlist instead of waiting around. I know he's innocent."

"Let's find out what's on that camera." He gave her a weak smile before turning the key in the ignition. Suddenly he heard Katie Mae calling from the front porch. She waved, then ran full speed toward the car, her blue dress flapping around her legs. He opened the power window and waited for her to reach them.

"Can you drive me into town?" she asked, hope glistening in her eyes. "I was about to hitch the horse to the buggy when *Mem* mentioned you were driving in." She squinted up at the sky. "Dark clouds are rolling in."

"*Mem* knows you're going with us?" Eli asked. He didn't want to be accused of being an undue influence on his little sister, even though many Amish were allowed to ride in cars. He hated to admit how much his father's words bothered him.

Katie Mae looked toward the house and waved, presumably to their mother who he imagined was standing at the kitchen window. His little sister jumped into the backseat of the car. "The fabric for my wedding dress is in at the general store."

Anna shifted in her seat. "When are you and Isaac getting married?"

Katie Mae's face grew bright red. The Amish did not talk

about engagements like people in the outside world. It was a formal matter to be taken seriously. It was not marked with wedding showers and bachelorette parties. "We haven't been published yet." Katie Mae adjusted the *kapp* on her head, the way she always did when she was nervous.

"The custom is for young Amish girls to make their own wedding dresses. So, Katie Mae is going to work on it well ahead of time to assure she's done when she and Isaac decide it's time." Eli looked into the rearview mirror and winked at his sister. He wished he could muster genuine enthusiasm for this union. He still thought of Isaac as the wild teenager who only recently returned to Apple Creek. He had since been baptized, but something about him bugged Eli.

What was Isaac thinking giving Samuel a radio?

Isaac still kept his car parked at an abandoned barn on the edge of Apple Creek. He claimed he didn't drive it, but Eli saw him once last month driving late at night. He put the car into gear and dismissed the thought. *Who am I to judge?*

"He's been courting me awhile." Katie Mae lowered her voice. "But we aren't supposed to talk about it. He visits me on Sunday evenings. That's where I was last night. He usually escorts me home from the singings." His little sister's face split into a wide grin, unable to hide her excitement. A bride was still a bride, he imagined. He, too, had been sweet on someone before Mary was kidnapped. He sometimes wondered what happened to Rebecca. Last he heard, she married a man from another Amish community and had a handful of children.

An unexpected emptiness tore at his soul. He realized something for the first time—he wanted a wife, children and something more in his life than this constant emptiness. He caught Anna's eye. A smile brightened her beautiful face and he was relieved she couldn't read his mind. Mentally shaking his head, he pulled onto the country road, doubting he'd find peace in anything until he found justice for Mary.

Once in town, Eli parked in a small lot between the general store and the diner. He picked a spot that didn't have a hitching post. He pushed open the door, thinking about how the past and the present fought for prominence in this small town. The past and present warred for position in his life, too. Katie Mae and Anna joined him around the back of the vehicle.

"After we stop in the general store, let's get something to eat at the diner," Eli said.

Katie Mae smiled. "Sounds good." She seemed especially cheerful today. Eli's chin dipped to his chest and he studied the ground. Should he speak up about his reservations about Isaac? Would his father even listen? Did he have any right to interfere with her future?

As always, when Eli went into the general store, the memories from that fateful day swept over him. Anna went to the counter and asked Mr. Lapp for AAA batteries while Katie Mae chatted happily with Mrs. Lapp, her future mother-in-law if all went as planned. After they made their purchases, they left the store, the bells clanking against the door and the sound jarring him. He had been too distracted the day Mary disappeared to hear any bells announcing anyone else's presence—or Mary's exit.

The three of them made an unlikely trio as they crossed the parking lot to the diner. They found a booth in the corner and placed their order. They were the only patrons in the diner, so Eli wasn't worried about hiding the camera. They sat quietly while Anna fidgeted with the camera for a few moments as she figured out how to load the batteries. He considered offering her help, but she seemed intent on the task.

Once the batteries were in place, she turned on the camera. A sense of anticipation charged the air. A quiet chime confirmed it had power. Anna glanced up, apprehension creasing her forehead. "I'm almost afraid to look."

"What are you looking at?" Katie Mae asked as the waitress returned to the table with three coffees.

"This is my brother's camera. I can scroll through the photos he took on it." The corners of Katie Mae's lips tugged down. "I'll show you in a minute."

Sitting next to Anna, Eli saw the digital display. Anna clicked a button and Tiffany's smiling face filled the screen. Then one of Daniel making a goofy face. Anna ran her finger over the glass. She scrolled through the photos. Images of farms and silos and silhouettes of Amish children flashed by. His claim that he was working on a book of Amish photographs seemed to be legitimate. Then an image filled the screen, and Eli inhaled sharply.

A photo of an Amish *kapp* in Daniel's hand.

"Stop," Eli said, his heart thumping in his chest. He took the camera and brought it to his face to examine the image. He clicked the zoom button. The *kapp* had jagged gray stitching around one edge. The handiwork had been done by a child. *My Mary.* Tears burned his throat. She had been so proud of the work, even when their mother corrected her for using the wrong shade of thread. But the little girl didn't care. It had been one of her first attempts at sewing.

But what brought him chills, even more than the familiar stitching, was the embroidery in the corner. *M.M.* His sister had carefully stitched her initials. The letters were surprisingly neat considering her age. Their mother had overlooked this minor transgression. Despite the fact that some Amish women sewed their initials on a handkerchief or corner of a dress pocket, which would be hidden by their apron, they would never monogram their *kapp*.

Lowering the camera, he looked over at his sister, who was sipping her coffee and watching him with interest. If he said anything now, Katie Mae would surely run home and tell their father and mother what he had found on the camera.

Anna's warm hand settled on his arm. He looked up and met her gaze. "Are you okay?" He nodded. Eli blinked a few times and scrolled through the photos. Prior to the image of the man holding his sister's *kapp* he had seen a series of photos of an old run-down cottage or cabin of some sort. He stared intently at the screen, wondering if Daniel had found his sister's *kapp* near the cabin.

"What's so interesting?" Katie Mae's voice came from over his shoulder. "Can I take a look?"

Eli tilted the camera so his sister could see the image of the cabin. He didn't want to shock her with the image of their little sister's *kapp*.

"My brother was taking photos of the countryside." Anna gave his forearm a reassuring squeeze. He wondered what she'd made out of her brother holding the *kapp*. Did she realize it was Mary's?

All sorts of questions crowded his mind. Where did Daniel find it? Was he going to implicate others? Where was it now? He rubbed his forehead. His mind raced.

"I know that cabin." Katie Mae startled him.

Leaning back, he looked up at his sister. She slid back into the booth across from him and took another sip of coffee. If not for the Amish clothing, her chattiness and excitement could have been mistaken for any other teenage girl in America. He wished for so much more for his sister. The world had a lot to offer her. He gritted his teeth. Who was he to brand one way of life better than another?

"You know where Daniel was when he took this photo?" he asked.

Katie Mae arched a pale eyebrow. "Yes. That's on the edge of the Christopher's lakefront property." She hitched a shoulder. "The one they use sometimes in the summer." She twisted her lips. "Never understood why people need two homes. The house they have in town could squeeze in all of the Millers and their cousins."

Eli's heart raced. Maybe this was the clue he had been working ten years to find. He struggled to keep his voice calm. "Is it next to the main house?" From looking at the photo, he couldn't imagine the Christophers would have allowed anything in their possession to have fallen into such disrepair.

"Oh, no…" Katie Mae's eyebrows shot up. "It's a good hike from the main house. One day in early spring, I had been put in charge of little Joey and Patrick, the Christopher's grandchildren, while their mother had her nails done. I tried to clean the house with them underfoot, but they had too much energy. I took them out for a walk and they kept going and going. Didn't even mind me when I called for them to come back. Lucky I kept up with them."

"This cabin is through the woods? Could you find it again?"

Katie Mae nodded. "It's near the lake. North of the main house."

"How do you know it's the same cabin?" Anna's brows drew together.

Katie Mae held out her hand and Eli handed over the camera. She squinted at the image, then handed it back, as if she were passing a hot potato. Perhaps she feared being seen in public with a camera. She pointed from a distance at the image. "See the broken railing?" Eli examined the photo. Sure enough, the horizontal rail was broken and resting at an angle. "I was thinking *Dat* would have fixed that rail the minute it broke."

Anxiety made it nearly impossible to stay seated in their small booth. He had to find this cabin and Mary's *kapp*. He fisted his hands.

He had to find Mary's body.

"You sure we're heading in the right direction?" Eli's deep voice broke the tension-filled silence.

"Yes." Katie Mae, her face inches from her backseat window, watched the scenery intently.

It was now late afternoon and Anna wished she hadn't pushed aside the hamburger at the diner. When Katie Mae had excused herself to use the bathroom, Eli had explained his suspicions about the bonnet—or *kapp* as he called it— leaving Anna nauseous. Now, a sinking feeling told her this wasn't going to be a quick trip to the cabin. She anticipated it as much as she dreaded it. Could this be the day they finally cleared her brother's name? Or the day the last nail was hammered into his coffin?

Coffin.

The cold word made all the blood rush from her head. She'd have to make arrangements for the proper burial of her brother's remains as soon as she returned home.

Up ahead, a dark purple-gray cloud moved in from the west, its edge pushing against the bright blue sky. A crack of lightning split the dark cloud. Anna counted. *Twenty-five.* A dull rumble sounded in the distance. A charge of anticipation tickled the back of her neck. Generally, she loved a good storm, but not today. She'd rather visit the rundown cabin under bright skies. She bit the inside of her cheek. Her stomach ached. Maybe she wasn't hungry after all.

Katie Mae tapped on the window, drawing Anna's attention again. Eli's sister sat in the seat behind her brother, an intense expression on her pale face. "Turn here. That narrow lane." Eli slowed and turned left onto a gravel road. Anna was impressed the young girl had remembered the directions.

As if answering her question, Katie Mae said, "We came down this lane and walked back on the side of the road. It was a lot quicker than trampling through the woods again. I had to get the boys home before their grandmother realized how far we had gone. I didn't want to lose my job." Katie Mae propped her elbow on the door and rested her chin on her fist. "I was hired to clean, not watch the kids. But Mrs. Christopher always seems overwhelmed when the grandchildren visit. And Chase's wife tends to bring the boys over to their grandparents' home a lot when Chase is traveling. Then she disappears, too."

Anna tapped her fingers on the center console, realizing they were getting close to the cabin in her brother's photos. As much as she wanted to clear his name, she feared finding something incriminating. What if witnessing their father murder their mother had shifted something in his personality? What if he had been warped enough to hurt a child? Eli reached over and covered her drumming fingers with his hand.

She cut him a sideways glance. "Sorry, I can't help it.'"

"Let's take it one step at a time, okay?" Eli smiled, the small gesture warming her heart.

Anna nodded, unable to form words. The tips of her fingers began to tingle and she sent up a silent prayer. *Dear Lord, please help me get through this.*

As they drove deeper into the woods, the thick canopy of tree branches swallowed them. The thick foliage and the clouds rolling in made it seem later than it really was. She ran a hand up and down her bare arms, wishing she had grabbed a sweater.

Up ahead a downed tree blocked the road. Eli slowed the vehicle and leaned forward, narrowing his gaze.

"We're going to have to park here and walk the rest of the way. It's not too far," Katie Mae said, pulling on the door handle.

They all climbed out of the SUV and assembled around front. Anna glanced down at her bare arms. She wasn't exactly dressed for a trek through the woods.

"We need to follow the road a little farther." Katie Mae hiked her dress and climbed over the thick tree trunk in the road. She strode ahead, as if on an adventure.

Eli grabbed Anna's hand. "Let's get moving. We don't have a lot of time. From the looks of it, rain is on the way." Without saying a word, Anna took his hand. He guided her over the tree and stuck close by as they trudged about a half mile. Anna tried not to make a big show of it, but every few feet she had to swat at the mosquitoes feasting on her flesh. Only Katie Mae chatted about this and that as they made their way deeper into the woods.

When they reached a small clearing, a cabin came into view. Large sections of roof tile were missing. A wicker chair sat upended in the yard. The railing was broken, like the one in the photo. Anna's knees grew weak. She was retracing Daniel's steps. Had they lead to his death?

The rich smell of damp soil reached her nose. The entire scene was dreary. She held her elbows tight to her sides and clasped her hands in front of her.

Eli's gaze swept over her. "You're getting eaten alive." He ran the back of his knuckle across her cheek. "There's even one here." His touch lingered. It was a completely innocent gesture, but she couldn't deny the growing attraction melting her insides. A smile played on his lips as if he knew the effect his touch had.

"I should have brought you back to my parents' house. You don't need to be out here."

"No, I'm fine."

He lifted a skeptical eyebrow. "Okay, let's go then." He started walking again and Anna followed. His sister had already reached the cabin. "Wait up, Katie. Don't go inside until I have a chance to check it out."

Nostalgia pulled at Anna's heart when she heard the protectiveness in Eli's voice. That's how Daniel had always been to her. Protective. Now it was her turn to look out for her big brother one final time, if only to protect his reputation.

"Don't be such a worrywart." Katie Mae climbed onto the porch and peered through the window. "No one's around." She had all the confidence of a young girl who had lived a very sheltered life. Now that Anna thought about it, it was a wonder her parents allowed her to have a job off the farm working for the Christophers. She thought the Millers would want to keep their only surviving daughter close at all times. But that wasn't the way they lived. She had heard something once from a devout Christian that worrying was showing your lack of faith in God. Anna fisted her hands and squeezed, wishing she could learn from them. Worrying was a favorite pastime of hers.

Visible through the small breaks in the branches, lightning continued to light up the sky. Thunder rumbled overhead. A rush of water rustled the leaves. Eli wrapped his arm around Anna's shoulders and started jogging. Katie waited for them under the porch's overhang. Head down, Anna ran alongside Eli, aware of his clean scent. Prior to Eli, she couldn't remember the last time she had been under the protective arm of a man. Her heart shifted. *Be careful,* a voice inside her head whispered. *This man has the power to destroy the reputation of the only family you ever really had.*

Anna shivered against Eli's arm. He squeezed her shoulder, the only physical contact he'd allow himself. As much as he sought justice for Mary, he feared finding his answers at the expense of this beautiful woman. Not exactly the foundation to build a relationship on. Glancing toward the cabin door, he found his sister staring at them with a huge smile.

"Excuse me." Eli dropped his arm from around Anna's shoulder and brushed past his sister. He tested the door handle. It was unlocked, which made things easier for him, but it also begged the question—who else had access? *Who didn't?* Teenagers probably used the deserted cabin as a hangout. "Wait here while I check things out."

Anna's eyes flared wide, as if she didn't trust him. Or did he detect a hint of fear? Her shoulders sagged in acquiescence. "Okay, but hurry." She swatted at something on her ankle. "I'm getting eaten alive out here."

He stepped into the cabin. The trapped stale air mixed with pine assaulted his nose. A few beer cans littered the table next to the couch. An opened bag of chips sat on the cushion. He walked over and picked them up. The expiration date on the bag was two weeks ago.

"Can we come in?" Katie called from the doorway.

"One sec." Eli did a quick sweep of the cabin, the two bedrooms, the bathroom and the closets. Whoever had been here wasn't here now. Perhaps Daniel had been the last person here. And they all knew what happened to him. Eli made his way back to the front door and pulled it wide open. "Come on in."

Katie Mae breezed into the room and flopped down on

the couch, the fabric of her full skirt landing in a swoosh. "I got a rock in my shoe." Yanking at her boot, she worked at the laces without much regard for anything else.

Anna stepped into the middle of the room, her thin arms around her middle. Her eyes grew wide as she took in her surroundings. He imagined she was thinking the same thing. Daniel had been here and he had Mary's *kapp*. Eli scrubbed a hand over his face, fearing the answers he had been so close to finding may now elude him forever.

"Where do we start?" Anna looked at him for guidance. He was about to answer when a huge clap of thunder made her jump. "Wow. That was close."

A torrential downpour pounded the roof while tree branches clawed at the walls. "We'll take our time here so we don't have to walk back through this weather."

"You don't think anyone will find us here trespassing?" Anna asked, concern lining her pretty features.

"Are you kidding?" Katie Mae spoke up. "The Christophers haven't used this place in years. I heard them say as much when their grandchildren asked about it." She lowered her voice. "Then they admonished the boys to never venture so deep in the woods. They said it wasn't safe." She pursed her lips. "And guessing from the way they take care of this place, I imagine they're right."

"We're fine," Eli reassured Anna. "I called Dr. Christopher, Chase's grandfather. He owns this property. He gave me permission to look around. Told me there's nothing but cobwebs at *that old place*."

Eli strode over to the kitchen and opened and closed drawers and cupboards. His stomach sloshed with dread. He half hoped and half feared he'd find Mary's *kapp*. But even if he did, what would it prove? Without saying a word, Anna strolled around the cabin, looking on bookshelves and under cushions.

Katie Mae busied herself picking up the empty beer cans. She held one to her nose and scrunched her face. "What are you guys looking for?"

Eli caught Anna's eye. "Something Daniel had."

Katie Mae didn't ask for clarification and went back to tidying up.

Anna approached Eli as he crouched and pulled out the contents of the closet in the bedroom. "You really don't think we'll find anything here, do you?"

Eli sat back on his heels and scratched his forehead. "I don't know what to think. Your brother obviously found my sister's *kapp*—" he looked over Anna's shoulder to make sure his sister was out of ear's reach "—and he was standing outside this cabin when he took a photo of it. I'm trying to put together the pieces."

"Maybe it was his form of insurance." Anna knelt down next to him. "He was afraid and by taking the photo, he wanted us to know he found the bonnet here." Anna looked at him with hopeful eyes. He knew she really wanted him to believe Daniel was innocent in all this. He wasn't convinced. Even if others had been involved, it didn't automatically make Daniel innocent.

Anna covered Eli's hand with hers. He flipped his hand over so their palms touched. His gaze lingered on her face. He leaned over and wiped at a black smudge on her cheek. "I wish we had met under different circumstances."

A small smile curved the corners of her pink lips. "Me, too."

Closing his eyes, he cupped her soft cheek and pressed his forehead against hers. "You think this was God's plan?" The scent of her fresh shampoo swirled around him.

She whispered, "I wish I knew His plan."

He savored the moment a fraction longer, then pulled away and helped her to her feet. "I've fallen away from my faith, but I want to believe God has good things in store for you."

Nodding, she averted her eyes. Pink colored her cheeks.

"Let's see if there's anything to be found in this place." He strode away, ignoring the pain evident in her hazel eyes.

THIRTEEN

Anna closed her eyes, willing away the swirling panic. The quiet moment she shared with Eli seemed like a dream. Now the musty smell permeating the rundown cabin made the walls close in. Breathing in and out slowly, she stood rooted in place.

Eli opened and closed the drawers in the dresser, each one banging shut a little louder. The frustration rolled off him in waves. "I don't know where to start," he muttered.

Anna sent up a silent prayer that the truth didn't mean destroying the warm feelings she had for her big brother. She wouldn't be able to live with that. Forcing a tight smile, an idea took shape. "The photo was taken outside with the cabin in the background. Maybe we should search outside." She flicked her gaze to the windows. Heavy rain sluiced down the panes, making it impossible to see outside. "If only it weren't raining."

"Hopefully it will let up soon." He sighed. "I'm afraid anything outside will be gone by now." Eli paced the space in front of the bed. "But Daniel had to find it someplace where it had been kept safe for ten years." A line creased his forehead. "Where would you hide something around here to keep it safe?"

Anna rubbed her cheek. "Floorboards. Attic. A secret compartment in the wall."

Eli turned from searching a cabinet along the wall and smiled at her. A twinkle lit his eyes, a welcome change from the intensity she had witnessed only moments ago. She shrugged, heat warming her cheeks at his slow perusal of her face. "I watch a lot of crime shows," she said in her defense.

"Nothing wrong with that." Eli strode out of the bedroom, tilting his face toward the ceiling. She did the same. No sign of an attic or a basement anywhere. He turned around and faced her. "We can't start tearing up the floorboards. I can't abuse Dr. Christopher's trust like that. Maybe if a few boards are loose, we can peek."

"Why would you have to tear the floorboards apart?" Katie Mae asked.

Eli hesitated, as if debating whether to tell his sister about Daniel's discovery. "Sit down, Katie."

The strings from her bonnet dangled around her chin. "No, you're scaring me." Her eyes grew bright. "Is this about Mary?"

Eli nodded.

"I knew it. That's what brought you back to Apple Creek." Katie's face grew paler.

He reached out and took his sister's hand. Anna stared as time slowed to a crawl. Eli's words came out even, calm. "Daniel took a photograph of Mary's *kapp*."

Katie Mae backed up and sat down on the sofa. Her brows snapped together. "How do you know it's hers? It could be anybody's."

"Remember when she tried to sew the seam herself and she added her initials?"

Katie Mae nodded but didn't say anything. The steady drum of rain slowed to a trickle.

"Let's go outside and get some air," Eli said, reaching for his sister's hand.

Anna heard him quietly ask his sister if she was all right. Katie Mae answered with a slow nod.

After the passing rain shower, dusk had gathered quickly, creating long shadows in the corners of the cabin's front porch. Katie Mae brushed at her skirt as if she was shaking away the dust.

The mud sucked at Anna's tennis shoes as she made her way across the property to where Eli stood. Anna turned around and framed the cabin in her sites. "I think Daniel must have been standing near here when he took that picture." Her brother loved nature. He loved capturing what other people tended to not see. But what had brought him all the way out here? What had led him to this cabin?

Eli searched the area. "The ground is wet but overall pretty solid. I don't see that anything was buried out here."

"If that *kapp* was Mary's, where is it now?" Katie glared at Anna accusingly.

"Exactly what I'm wondering." Eli seemed to be picking his words carefully. "Why didn't your brother turn it in immediately?"

"He feared it would make him look guilty." The words tumbled out one after the other. That was the only explanation that made any sense.

Eli ran a hand across his mouth. "He had the chance when he met with me. But he didn't. Or he could have called the sheriff."

The sheriff's smug face came to mind. "He didn't like the sheriff."

"I imagine that's true. The sheriff came down hard on him ten years ago."

Anna planted her fists on her hips. "The sheriff investigated a lot of fraternities in town the day Mary disappeared. The only reason he focused on my brother was because of the rumors surrounding my parents' deaths."

Her anger heated her ears. "My father's wrath infected my family long after his death."

"Okay, we do know your brother had Mary's *kapp*." He shifted his weight and seemed to be taking in the surroundings. "Where is it now?"

Anna swatted at another mosquito.

"I think I saw bug spray near the sink." Katie Mae had strolled to the edge of the clearing and was staring at the lake. A few rays of sun poked through the clouds close to the horizon.

"Be careful near that cliff, Katie Mae," Eli called. His sister nodded and moved back from the edge.

Going insane from the itching, Anna started to walk toward the house. "I'll be right back." She couldn't figure out why the bugs weren't bothering Eli or Katie Mae. She supposed it was because she had the most exposed flesh. She scratched at her arms and her ankles. It was maddening.

The first porch step creaked under Anna's weight. Once again, when she opened the cabin door, the thick musty smell assaulted her. It seemed the shadows had grown longer in the short interval since they had left. A shiver crawled across her skin. She glanced over her shoulder and saw the beam of light from Eli's flashlight bouncing around the property. Nightfall was coming fast. Pushing back her shoulders she swatted at yet another mosquito and made her way inside. It would only take a second. In and out.

Anna stepped into the room and stopped. Her heartbeat kicked up a notch. She had the distinct sense she wasn't alone. She backed up and reached for the doorknob. A figure emerged from the shadows on the other side of the room. With a sweat-slicked palm, she tried to turn the door handle but her hand slipped off. She tried to scream but couldn't find her voice.

Dear Lord, help me.

The figure stood there, staring at her, but she couldn't make out his features in the darkened room. He made a sudden move toward her. Against the dim light filtering in through the windows, she discerned the distinct shape of a hat with a broad brim. She stood transfixed, her legs like jelly, before she willed herself to move. She bolted toward the back exit. Dizzy from the surge of adrenaline, she leaned heavily on the door. Her fingers found the handle and she yanked it open.

Thank God.

She stepped onto the back porch and ran to a nearby crop of trees, trying to determine the best path to make her way around to Eli. Footsteps on the back porch made her blood run cold. She dipped behind a tree and crouched down. *Dear Lord, please protect me.* She squeezed her eyes shut. *Watch over Eli and Katie Mae.*

Silence stretched for what seemed like an eternity. She lifted her head, her rasping breaths joining the cacophony of night critters. An explosion ripped through the night air. She buried her face in her arms. A searing heat whooshed across the back of her neck. Her heart plummeted. *Oh, no.*

Orange flames shot out the windows, consuming the cabin in greedy licks.

An explosion made Eli spin around. Icy dread coursed through his veins when he saw the cabin in a ball of fire. *Anna!*

Katie Mae had flattened herself against a tree, a hand over her mouth. He clutched his sister's arms. "Are you okay?" Katie nodded. The flames reflected in her terror-filled eyes. "Stay here. Don't move. Do you understand?"

Katie Mae nodded.

Breaking into a full run, he approached the front of the cabin. The heat from the fire pushed him back. The bright glow of the flames made the surrounding area black as night. He heaved from the exertion. Adrenaline pumped through his veins. "Anna! Anna!" he screamed.

No answer. The entire woods had turned silent.

Black smoke clogged his lungs. Bending at his waist, he braced his hands on his knees. His pulse thrummed in his ears. He strained to hear. He wanted something—anything —to indicate Anna was okay.

Okay, God. I haven't come to You for much lately, but if You are really out there, I need You now. Don't let me down. Please send Anna safely to me.

The crackling of dried beams split the night air. The cabin was going up like a tinderbox. No way could anyone survive.

Please God.

Panic made his heart race. Frantically, he pointed his flashlight to the black edges of the yard. He strode around to the side of the cabin, searching for an alternate way in. The beam from his flashlight bounced off a side window.

"Anna! Anna!"

Exploding glass made him jump back. The flames licked the edges of the window.

Please God, help Anna escape. Help me find her in time.

Despite the roaring in his ears a calmness descended upon him. He strode around the back of the cabin as if driven by some unseen hand. He had to push aside overgrown shrubs and low tree branches to make his way to the back door.

A twig snapped and he whirled his flashlight around. Anna stepped out from behind a tree, and she held a hand up to block the beam from his flashlight. Relief flooded his system. He pulled her into a fierce embrace. Glancing up, he whispered, "Thank You, God." He leaned back to look at her. The oranges flames glinted in the whites of her eyes. "You are okay, aren't you?"

Anna nodded and buried her face in his chest. "I got out before the explosion. I hid behind a tree."

The taste of charred wood coated his dry mouth. *Thank you.*

"What happened?" He traced her cheek with the pad of his thumb. Tears left tracks on her sooty face.

"There was a man in there." She swiped a hand across her wet cheek. "He ran toward me, but I got around him and escaped out the back door."

Eli ran a protective hand down her arm. "Did he touch you?"

"No." Her fair skin glistened from the heat of the fire.

His eyes drifted toward the inferno. "I didn't notice anyone leaving through the front."

"No, he followed me out the back. That's why I hid." She released a long shaky breath. "Hiding probably spared me getting hurt from the explosion."

"I shouldn't have brought you here." Obviously someone wanted them to stop investigating Mary's disappearance. He couldn't live with losing someone he cared about. *Not again.* The realization nearly knocked the wind out of him.

Anna narrowed her gaze. "I wanted to come with you, remember? I have as much at stake as you do."

Shaking his head, he plucked his cell phone from his back pocket. No signal. *Figures.* "We'll have to hike back to the car and get help. You think you can manage?" Anna took a step, testing her legs. He grabbed her elbow to steady her, his gaze scanning the darkened woods around them. *Katie Mae.* Sweat trickling down between his shoulder blades, he strode as fast as he could, guiding Anna by her elbow. He sent up a silent prayer of thanks when he saw Katie Mae standing exactly where he had left her.

"What happened?" Katie Mae's whisper was barely audible over the crackling of the timber.

"Do you think we should look for a hose? I'd hate for the trees to go up," Anna said.

"No, we wouldn't stand a chance with a hose. I hope the drenching rain we had earlier will buy us time to call the fire department."

Eli held Anna's forearm tightly as they made their way down the path. He kept his flashlight beam pointed ahead, aware of his sister leading the way. The weight of his gun in its holster provided a measure of comfort. Whoever did this hadn't gone far. They were probably still in the woods nearby. Watching them. If they had been desperate enough to blow up the cabin, they wouldn't hesitate to come after them as they made their way across the rutted path to his vehicle.

A million stars dotted the sky as Eli climbed out of his SUV. He had called the fire department as soon as he had gotten cell phone reception—which happened to be where the car was parked. Then they stopped at the sheriff's station to give a full report. Eli told Katie Mae not to tell their parents about Mary's *kapp*. He didn't want his parents to worry and he didn't want the information to get out. Not yet, anyway.

After seeing Anna and Katie Mae safely home, he drove to the closest neighbors with a landline. He didn't have the patience to drive back into town to get cell phone reception. He made a few quick phone calls to work associates in Buffalo, then rushed back to his parents' house, uneasy that he had left Anna out of his sight.

He slipped off his mud-caked shoes at the back door and gave his mother a weary smile.

Mariam looked up from her meal preparations. "She's

upstairs cleaning up." His mother answered his unasked question. "Katie Mae told me there was a fire?" Her brow furrowed in confusion.

"It's a long story, *Mem*. But I'm going to take Anna somewhere else to stay. It's too dangerous for her here." His hand instinctively went to his gun. He could protect himself. Now he had to protect Anna. Someone didn't want them to uncover the truth. "I'm afraid staying here isn't a good idea." He glanced around the tidy but plain kitchen, starting to understand how the simple life left room for so much more. His job—his responsibilities—weighed heavily on him. "I can't do that to you and Father. You've already been through so much."

Mariam placed the wooden spoon down on the counter and turned around slowly. "I already spoke with your father. You must stay as long as you are in town." His father would have never extended the offer personally, but his mother's words spoke volumes.

Eli rubbed the back of his neck. He had already called in a few friends from Buffalo to provide extra security. Whether he and Anna stayed here or not, he wanted someone keeping an eye on his parents' property. No one was going to get to his parents' house without raising a red flag.

"Thanks." Eli patted his mother's hand and she met his gaze with a tired smile. "Maybe it would be best if I kept an eye on things here, too. I'm going to check on Anna."

Eli climbed the stairs and stopped outside Anna's bedroom. The soft glow from the lamp flickered through the crack underneath the door. He knocked quietly. He heard a muted shuffling, then saw a shadow under the door. A second later, her clean, pale face shone up at him. Her hair was wrapped in a white towel, and she had on a T-shirt and gray pajama bottoms.

Feeling his face redden—something he wasn't accustomed to—he stepped back. "I'm sorry. I wanted to make sure you were okay."

Anna stepped aside and held out her arm, welcoming him into her room. He crossed over to the window. Under the bright moon, he could see the landscape. The barn loomed as an imposing figure across the yard. Someone had been stalking Anna from its loft. Despite his mother's insistence, maybe staying here wasn't the best idea. Indecision dogged him. He glanced down at his cell phone for the time. His reinforcements should be here soon.

He turned around to face Anna. Something he didn't dare acknowledge stirred in his heart, but he dismissed it as his protective instinct. Nothing more. "I talked to the chief of the fire department. They have the fire contained. He thinks one of the propane tanks on the back porch blew."

Anna nodded but didn't say anything. "There's something I didn't tell you."

Eli narrowed his gaze. She sat on the corner of the bed. "The person I saw…"

"The person in the cabin?"

"Yes." The look in Anna's eyes was tentative. She seemed to be searching for the right words. "I didn't want to say anything in front of Katie Mae, but he's Amish."

A pounding started behind Eli's eyes. He slumped against the windowsill. "Why do you think that?"

Anna pulled the white towel from her head. Her curly hair spilled out around her shoulders, leaving wet spots on her dark-blue T-shirt. "I saw the outline of his—" She touched the crown of her head. "It had a brim, like the hats the Amish wear."

Eli pushed a hand through his hair. "That can't be." Anna met him with an unwavering stare but didn't say anything. "The Amish don't believe in violence. They are conscientious objectors. They never resort to violence." He realized the ridiculousness of this generalization. The Amish were people, too, who made good and bad choices. They had free will, just like everyone else.

"I'm just telling you what I saw," Anna said through gritted teeth.

"Maybe in the confusion…" He stopped arguing when he met her steely gaze of determination.

"The person in the cabin was wearing an Amish hat." She lowered her voice. "Maybe he wanted me to think he was Amish." Narrowing her gaze, she seemed deep in thought. "But I don't think he was expecting me. I surprised him. Maybe I'm grasping at straws, but I think he was looking for something." She scratched absentmindedly at a red mark on her arm. "Who knew we were going to the cabin?"

"Only Dr. Christopher. Chase's grandfather. I called him. He's a good man. When he was still practicing medicine, he often treated the Amish for little or no fee. He owns the property and I wanted his permission to search it in case we found anything. Otherwise, if we found evidence, we wouldn't be able to use it in a court of law."

"Why would he give his permission?"

Eli shrugged. "I suppose he didn't think we'd find anything."

Anna nodded slowly. "Maybe Dr. Christopher told someone…or someone overheard the conversation."

Eli rubbed his jaw. "Tom Hanson lives with him. I'll talk to him."

Anna stood and crossed to the window. The scent of her hair coiled through him and against his better judgment, he took a step closer. The only indication she was aware of his proximity was the faint blush of pink blossoming up her neck. She stared out the window, her arms hanging loosely at her sides. He reached out and twirled a wet strand of hair around his fingers. Boldly, he cupped her cheek with his other hand and turned her face toward his.

"You scared me today," he whispered, his voice hoarse.

A thin line, barely visible in the flickering glow of the soft light, creased her forehead. He traced the line with his finger, then let it drop to the softness of her cheek. "I reached out to God when I couldn't find you during the fire."

A small smile played on her lips.

He lowered his gaze before lifting it to meet hers. "Sometimes He does answer our prayers."

She blinked slowly as his finger moved down to tilt her chin. Leaning in, he brushed his lips chastely against hers, testing her resolve. He pulled back and studied her face. Her dark lashes rested against her pale cheeks.

Under different circumstances.

Something stirred deep within him. She smelled of lotion and soap. Her freshly scrubbed face had never been more beautiful.

It was Anna who broke the spell swirling around them. She bowed her head, then stepped back from his touch. She crossed her arms over her T-shirt, as if embarrassed. "We're both under a lot of stress." Her clear hazel eyes locked with his. He wanted to tell her it was more than that. That he had started to care for her deeply. But could she ever trust him when he still had doubts about her brother's involvement with Mary's disappearance?

"Anna—"

A rapping at the door startled them. They stepped guiltily apart. "Come in," Anna said, her voice scratchy.

The door creaked open. Abram stood in the doorway, a stern look on his face. He waited for his father's scolding as if he were a teenager again. But the scolding never came. "Two men are downstairs. I believe you called for them."

* * *

Anna followed Eli downstairs, her hand skimming the top of the railing. Lightheaded, she didn't trust her legs to support her. The sweet sensation from his tender kiss had affected her like no other. Could she be falling for this man? She didn't even want to imagine that complication. Maybe her emotions stemmed more from loneliness now her only family was gone. She hated that needy part of her. She had always been so independent.

Unexpected longing twisted around her heart. Wouldn't it be nice to have someone to rely on? She rubbed her temples. Her thoughts suddenly shifted. Someone to let her down? To hurt her? To leave her?

At the bottom of the stairs, two men dressed in jeans and dark golf shirts greeted Eli. He shook their hands and introduced them to Anna and Abram. Abram didn't appear too welcoming.

"I invited Dominic and William to help me keep an eye on things," Eli said, his gaze trained on his father.

Abram hiked his chin. "We have had enough of the outside world to last us a lifetime." Cutting his gaze toward his son, he continued, "This is my home. You should have asked before you invited these men here."

Eli stared resolutely at his father. "You would have said no."

"Then I think you'd understand why I find this disrespectful. You have never respected our ways. You made that abundantly clear when you left Apple Creek. You can continue your way of life but not under my roof. If you ever decide to join us fully in baptism, we will welcome you with open arms." Abram's tone was sharp, angry. Although he had always been stern, Anna had never heard him raise his voice. Out of the corner of her eye, she noticed Eli wince.

"Father, I respect your position. However, Dominic and

William are with a private security firm. I have hired them to patrol the premises until we can figure out who has been trying to hurt Anna." Eli slid his hand across the small of her back. She resisted the urge to lean into him, to find strength in him. "I promise you they will not interfere with your way of life." Eli seemed to pick his words carefully.

Abram's mouth flattened into a grim line and his shoulders shifted. It seemed as though he might walk away without saying anything more. She sensed this was how Eli's father dealt with his rebel son. Guilt and silence. Didn't these men know they were the only family they'd ever have?

It was then that Mariam stepped into the foyer. "I have trust in God to protect my family. I also trust Eli knows what's best in this situation." She looked at her husband, pleading with her eyes. "If he deems it's necessary to have these two men here as extra eyes and ears against the evil that is out there, I ask you to please reconsider, Abram." Anna detected fear in Mariam's voice.

"The small bedroom near the back of the house is available for when they need to rest. It's not much, but it has a cot." Abram turned and walked away.

"Thanks," Eli called after his father. Lowering his voice, he added, "I respect your home, *Mem*. Dominic and William will rotate rounds. I want to make sure my family is safe."

Anna's heart tightened in her chest from a twinge of jealousy. Even though he was estranged from them, he still had a family to protect.

Mariam retreated to the back of the house to join her husband. Mariam had effectively gotten her way while still deferring to her husband. Anna hung back, her arms crossed over her T-shirt, suddenly feeling very conspicuous, as Eli walked outside with Dominic and William. But curiosity got the best of her. She stepped out onto the porch and listened to the men talk. It was decided they would both watch the property but then alternate shifts when they got tired.

Clutching the hem of her shirt, she scanned the darkened yard. Was someone out there now? Watching? An idea slammed into her and she found herself forcing her shoulders back. Her comment would have to wait. She didn't know these two new men and didn't want to share her thoughts in front of them.

A horse neighed loudly near the road. Squinting, Anna made out the outline of a wagon turning toward the house. The Amish man hopped off and Anna tracked his movements as he strode toward them. The image from the cabin of a man—Amish hat perched on his head—solidified in her imagination. Should she be suspicious of all Amish men? The idea seemed preposterous. There must be hundreds of men in this community alone who wore these wide-brimmed hats.

She found herself stepping back, ready to retreat into the house. She glanced at the three strong men standing next to her, guns strapped to their bodies. If she couldn't feel safe now, would she ever? Maybe if she went home…? Away from whatever danger lurked here in Apple Creek.

She couldn't run forever.

Dominic was the first to come down the steps, one hand hovering over the handle of his gun. Anna's heart jackhammered in her chest. Eli seemed to shift, blocking her view, a protective gesture. "Hold up, there," Dominic said in a deep voice, one that commanded authority.

"What's this all about?" Anna recognized the male voice. She peered around Eli to see Isaac leaning casually on the post at the bottom of the steps. "Something else going on I don't know about?" A look of amusement graced his narrow face as the corners of his mouth quirked into a grin.

"Isaac, we have a lot going on here. Maybe you can pay a social visit to my sister another time." Eli crossed his arms over his broad chest.

Isaac cocked his head in obvious confusion. "Samuel came running over and left a message with *Mem* about some kind of accident. That Katie Mae was shaken up. You can't tell me I can't see Katie Mae."

A muscle worked in Eli's jaw, but Anna doubted Isaac noticed. He seemed to be filled with more self-confidence than the other Amish men she had met in the community. Maybe his hubris stemmed from his experience in the outside world. Worldliness the other Amish men lacked. Worldliness he'd have to lose if he wanted to fit in with these humble people.

A niggling tugged at the base of Anna's brain. She prayed Katie Mae came to her senses before she settled down with Isaac. Surely there was someone better suited for her.

Eli glanced toward the house, then stepped aside. "I'll tell Katie Mae you're here." Apparently this was not a battle he wanted to take on.

Dominic and William brushed past Isaac and strode toward their vehicles, out of place on this farm time had forgotten. Presumably they were going to devise a plan on how to protect the Millers' home—and her. A sour taste made her flinch. Her gaze drifted to the cornfields across the road, but all she could see was darkness.

"So," Isaac said in a lazy lilt, "I hear the Christophers' cabin went up in ball of fire." His lips tugged down at the corners, but his eyes seemed bright, intrigued. "You narrowly escaped?"

Anna regarded him quietly, her eyes moving to his hat. Anger bubbled up quite unexpectedly. "What do you know about it?"

Isaac frowned and cupped his hands over his chest as if he were offended. "Only what Samuel shared with me. He said you almost got blown up while Katie Mae and Eli were outside."

The memory of the flames licking at the back of her neck made the fine hairs stand on edge. "I'm all right now. Thanks for asking." She hated the bristle in her voice. Maybe this was Isaac's way. He reminded her of a bored gossip.

A moment later, Eli returned, holding open the screen door. "Katie Mae's in the kitchen."

Isaac tipped his hat at Anna, then went inside. Anna rubbed her arms, trying to dispel the coolness of the evening. "Do you think…"

"What?" Eli pressed.

"Do you think Katie Mae will be happy with Isaac? She seems so innocent and he's… I can't put my finger on it."

Eli's eyes shimmered in the moonlight and a deep rumble of laughter filled the night air. She couldn't help but giggle in response. The day's events had made her punchy. "What's so funny?" Her cheeks grew warm.

"He's always rubbed me the wrong way, too. I figured I was being the overprotective big brother." Eli playfully ran the palm of his hand along her forearm, her flesh tingling under his touch.

She shrugged. "He unnerves me." She lowered her voice to barely a whisper. "What's his story?"

"You already know he's been courting Katie Mae for almost a year now. I imagine sometime soon they'll be publishing their engagement." His tone was solemn. She supposed it frustrated him he had little say in what happened in his sister's world.

"He seems much older than she."

"He is. He's my age. He left the Amish way of life for

a few years. Came back I'd say eighteen months ago." Eli took Anna's hand and led her to one of the straight-back chairs on the porch. She slowly sat down, the cool wood chilly through her thin pajama bottoms.

"And he was welcomed back? Just like that?" Anna snapped her fingers. "I thought the Amish were strict."

"Oh, they are." Eli ran his palms along the smooth arms of the chair. "But if you repent, if you ask for forgiveness, they will welcome you back. Haven't you been listening to my parents? They lay the guilt on thick, hoping eventually their methods will wear me out. That I'll return and be baptized." He leaned toward her. She smelled the subtle mix of charred wood and his aftershave. Her stomach did a little flip flop at his proximity. "A family welcomes back a wayward son, relieved he now has a shot at eternal salvation."

"Has a shot?"

"Ah, the Amish do not assume salvation is guaranteed. They are a humble people. But the best chance of going to heaven is living a good life within the rules of the Amish church or the Ordnung."

"Did you really reach out to God today?" Anna asked, keeping her gaze trained on the darkened yard.

"Yes." Eli let out a long breath. "Maybe you can teach an old dog new tricks." She detected a smile in his voice.

Closing her eyes, she pushed her feet against the wood planks, making the chair move in a subtle back and forth motion. Was her faith as strong as she proclaimed? Had she truly trusted God to lead her through this troubled time? Where did she stand when it came to eternal life?

What if I had met my maker today in the explosion?

FOURTEEN

The next morning, Anna got up early, unable to sleep. She rolled out of bed and pulled back the curtain. Orange and pink streaked the country sky, promising a beautiful day—at least in the weather department. Her burdensome worries already weighed her down.

Trust God.

She sat down on the edge of her bed and shrugged, shaking off the chill of the early morning. Footsteps and clattering dishes indicated the Miller women were up and preparing for the day. A twinge of shame jabbed her. She felt lazy stretching and wiping the sleep out of her eyes. She missed her quiet apartment. The solitude in the morning. The time to pull herself together before she had to face other people.

She wished she had the freedom to go for a morning run, but she knew that was out of the question. It wasn't safe and besides, she needed to rest after her concussion. She smoothed a hand over her mussed hair. Would returning to Buffalo be an end to her troubles? Wasn't that what someone wanted? For her to go home and stop pushing this investigation?

Yet Eli would continue to push.

She did have to return to her job in Buffalo. Her students

were counting on her, and they were approaching the end of the first marking quarter. She sighed heavily, wondering what had happened to the bonnet in the photo. Dread snaked its way through her body. She pushed back her shoulders in quiet determination. She had to stick it out a few more days and help Eli clear her brother's name, realizing Eli's goal was not necessarily to clear her brother's name, but to find his sister's kidnapper.

Getting down on her knees and resting her elbows on the quilt, she closed her eyes and tried again. *Dear Lord, help me do right by my brother. Please bring closure for the Miller family. May they find peace in knowing what happened to their dear Mary. I will work hard to trust Your plan. Amen.*

Anna swiped at a tear trailing down her cheek. She pushed to her feet. A thin rim of orange peaked over the trees in the distance. She watched silently as the sun rose higher in the sky. Grabbing jeans and a T-shirt out of her suitcase, she tiptoed to the bathroom to get ready for the day. She ran a brush through her wet hair, then checked her face in the mirror. She looked pale without her makeup but otherwise fine. She smoothed balm on her lips and headed downstairs.

She found Katie Mae cooking at the kitchen stove. "Morning," Anna said.

Katie Mae looked up with a pinched expression on her face. Without saying a word, she gave Anna her back and returned to stirring something on the stove. The curt greeting left Anna unsettled. She glanced out the window. In the driveway sat one of the cars of the men who had arrived to protect her. She figured he couldn't be far.

"Isaac thinks it's time you left." Katie Mae's quiet, angry words cut through the silence.

Anna turned around and found Eli's little sister glaring

at her. The oatmeal from her spoon plopped onto the hard-wood floor. "Your parents invited me to stay." She understood Katie Mae's concern but couldn't figure out why she had turned on her overnight. Maybe the explosion at the cabin had profoundly affected her.

Katie Mae frowned and tossed the spoon into the pot, then stepped toward Anna. She spoke in a hushed voice. "That is their way. They don't like confrontation." Katie pointed at one of the men, now leaning on his vehicle. "You have brought these men here who are patrolling our peaceful farm." She lowered her eyes. "We all could have been killed in the explosion."

"I'm sorry." Anna rubbed her temples. The first hint of a headache scraped across her brain. "I wish I knew who was behind this."

"Isaac thinks things would go back to normal if you went away."

A fire grew in her chest. "What do *you* think, Katie Mae?"

Katie Mae looked Anna in the eyes, the spark no longer there. "Isaac says your brother took our Mary. He doesn't understand why Eli doesn't declare the case closed now that your brother's gone."

Katie Mae's words pierced her heart like a dagger. "What do you think?" Anna repeated, this time more softly.

The girl crossed to the kitchen table, pulled out a chair and dropped down. She fingered the strings on her bonnet, then folded her hands in her lap. After what appeared to be an internal struggle, Eli's sister looked up at her, an apology in her eyes. "I like you, Anna. You are good for my brother...I was so scared yesterday."

Anna sat across from Katie Mae. "You and me both."

"Eli is driven. He won't rest until he finds out what happened to Mary." The young woman bowed her head. "I am more like my parents. I have forgiven whoever did this. I want to move forward." A tiny smile graced Katie Mae's pale lips. "I don't believe your brother had anything to do with my Mary. He's your family and if he was anything like you, it's not possible. You are so kind."

Anna's heart felt full. "Thank you."

"Besides, that would just complicate things between you and *my* brother." Katie Mae's chin dipped down. "I see how he looks at you."

Nerves tangled in Anna's belly. "Eli and I have bigger concerns than worrying about our relationship." A quiet laugh escaped her lips. "The only relationship we have is to find out what my brother was doing in Apple Creek." She reached across and touched Katie Mae's hand. "You were nine when Mary disappeared?"

Katie Mae nodded, pulling her hand away from Anna's and folding them in her lap. "Oh, Mary loved Eli. Tagged along with him everywhere."

"I felt the same way about my brother." She fought the threatening tears. "I have to believe he's innocent."

Katie Mae smiled, a tenderness touching her eyes. "I hope you find what you're looking for."

Heavy footsteps on the back porch drew their attention. Katie Mae jumped to her feet and started stirring the oatmeal. "The men will be coming in from their morning chores for breakfast."

Anna stood. "Can I help you?"

A small smile flitted at the corners of Katie Mae's mouth. She gestured with her elbow to the fruit sitting on the counter. "Can you cut the cantaloupe?"

Anna picked up the sharp knife and cut through the melon on the wood cutting board. She was surprised to see Eli stroll in, sweat glistening off his forehead. She had assumed he was still in bed. Hay stuck to his T-shirt. A few tufts of hair stood up. Warmth blossomed in her chest, and Katie Mae's words floated back to her: *I see the way he looks at you.*

"You got up early." She returned her attention to slicing the melon.

"Thought I'd get my morning workout in and help with chores. Kill two birds with one stone." His voice sounded husky this morning.

Her heart fluttered and heat warmed her face. She focused intently on cutting the fruit into small slices. Samuel stomped in behind his older brother. He tossed his hat on a hook by the door. Katie Mae made a shooing gesture. "Go clean up for breakfast."

Eli passed by, brushing his hand gently across her arm. She froze with the knife poised above the fruit, trying to quell her rioting emotions. She looked up to find Katie Mae staring, her mouth sloped in an I-told-you-so expression.

Anna's face was on fire. Things had gotten far too complicated in this supposedly simple world.

Eli plunked down at the breakfast table—in the same seat he had sat in as a child. He glanced up to find two sets of expectant eyes on him. He had the niggling sense he had walked in on a conversation he wasn't supposed to hear. Katie Mae had a faint smile on her lips. She filled a coffee mug and handed it to Anna. "I believe Eli likes his coffee black."

Eli bit back a smile of his own when he noticed Anna's confused look. She cut a sideways glance to his sister, who then nudged her gently toward Eli. Anna gave a slow nod in understanding, then walked over and set the coffee mug down, the ceramic clanking against the pine table, the dark contents swishing out the sides. She lifted a perfectly groomed brow. "Don't get used to this," she said, barely above a whisper. A twinkle lit her eye.

He reached out and brushed his hand across hers. "Oh, I could."

Leaning close so her long curls brushed his shoulder, she whispered close to his ear. "You live in the English world now, buddy."

He reached up and gently yanked on a curl, releasing the fresh coconut scent of her shampoo. Her hazel eyes widened and she stepped back, her hair slipping out of his fingers. He winked at her. He woke up this morning so incredibly grateful that Anna hadn't been hurt—or worse—yesterday in the fire. Now, he wondered more than ever if, after this mess was cleared up, they had a shot at getting to know one another better. It seemed like the fates had a horrible sense of humor if they conspired for him to fall for Anna.

The fates? A quiet voice whispered across his brain. *Perhaps you should put more faith in God.*

A pounding at the front door snapped him out of his reverie. He pushed back from the table and held out a protective arm to stop Anna and his sister. "Let me get it." Ignoring him, Anna followed him to the front door, where they found the sheriff. Dominic, one of the security guards, stood nearby at the bottom of the porch steps.

"What's going on, Sheriff?" Eli asked. Anna slipped her hand around the bend of his arm.

The sheriff focused his narrowed eyes on Anna. "We need to talk to her."

"About what?" Eli covered Anna's hand and squeezed.

"It seems the fire at the Christopher cabin was arson."

Anna straightened her back. "I already told you I saw someone in the cabin before the explosion."

The sheriff tipped his hat. "Are you sticking to your story?"

"I—" Anna started to protest when Eli squeezed her hand in a gentle warning.

"Is Anna in some kind of trouble? Does she need a lawyer?" Eli recognized a fishing expedition. He didn't understand the sheriff's angle. This went beyond the usual turf war between locals and the FBI.

The sheriff took the slightest step back, indicating he wasn't ready to make an arrest. "You might want to call yourself a lawyer, Miss Quinn."

A quiet gasp escaped her lips. "It's okay," Eli whispered.

The sheriff reached into his pocket and pulled out a plastic bag. Inside was a gold item. Anna reached for it with a shaky hand, but the sheriff pulled back the bag. "You recognize this, Miss Quinn?"

Anna looked up at Eli, helplessness reflected in her eyes. "It's my mother's lighter."

"Any idea how your mother's lighter ended up in the charred ruins of the Christopher cabin?"

Eli spoke first. "Anna did *not* set that fire. I was there. She barely escaped the explosion when the propane tank went." The memory of the fireball twisted his insides. "No way."

The sheriff tipped his head. "Are you sure? How well do you know her?"

Eli didn't like the way he said the word *her.* "I know Anna Quinn well enough. She'd have no reason…" A hint of doubt whispered across his brain. *To protect her brother. To destroy any possible evidence in the cabin?* But risk her own life? She had already escaped out the back of the cabin.

"No way," he repeated.

The sheriff stuffed the lighter in his pocket. "We got a solid print off the lighter. I've contacted the State Department of Education." He smiled smugly at Anna. "I'm checking to see if your employment fingerprints are still on file."

"But…" Anna seemed to struggle to find words. "I saw a man with an Amish hat run out the back of the cabin before it exploded."

"Convenient. You know how many men around here are Amish?" The sheriff turned on his heel and walked down the steps. "Besides, they sell those hats down at the general store. *If* you actually saw someone else there."

Anna's face grew ashen white. "Why would I blow up a cabin?" She threaded her fingers through the ends of her hair. "My hair got singed. Why would I almost kill myself in the process?"

The sheriff turned around. "To hide evidence that proves your brother kidnapped and murdered Mary Miller."

Eli swallowed back his revulsion. "What are you talking about?"

"Isaac told us about the photos of Mary's bonnet. He also said you were alone in the cabin before it went up." The sheriff cocked an eyebrow.

Eli gritted his teeth. A cold rage welled up inside him. Katie Mae must have fed Isaac all sorts of information. "I think Anna knows more than she's letting on."

"No, that's—" Anna started to protest and Eli held up his hand to stop her.

"Sheriff, I was there. Anna did not start the fire." He tried to tamp his anger simmering under the surface. "Don't bother coming back here unless you have an arrest warrant." Eli wrapped his arm around Anna's shoulder and pulled her close.

"Trust me, I will," the sheriff hollered over his shoulder. "I told you the Quinns were nothing but bad eggs. If I were a betting man, I'd say she knows what her brother hid up there at the cabin and destroyed the evidence before we had a chance to find it."

The sheriff strolled over to his cruiser and climbed in.

He made a show of taking a few notes before turning his vehicle around and leaving. Anna sagged against him. He ran his hand down the length of her arm. "Don't worry. He's full of bluster." He forced a smile in a display of levity he didn't feel.

How well do I know Anna?

As if reading his doubts, Anna slipped away from him and dropped into the rocker on the porch. She slumped against its hard back. He crossed to her and leaned back against the rail. She looked up, steely resolve mixed with something he couldn't quite name glistening in her eyes. "My fingerprints are on that lighter."

Eli narrowed his gaze. "There are probably a million fingerprints on it. How long ago did your mother pass away?"

"No, you don't understand. I touched it recently."

Anna's heart beat wildly as Eli parked his SUV in front of Daniel's garage apartment. The last time she had seen her mother's lighter was at Daniel's place a few days ago. Someone must have come in after them and taken the lighter from the table next to his couch.

Tom Hanson met them in the driveway. Eli slammed the car door shut and towered over Tom. "Anyone else stop by? Who else has a key to this apartment?"

Tom lowered his eyes, then quickly glanced toward the street. "I have another one on the key ring. And the last renter never returned the key when he moved out." He shrugged. "Who knows how many keys are floating around out there? It's not like we have a high crime rate. Most people don't even lock their doors around here."

"I locked it after Anna and I left. You go back in there?"

"No and as far as I know, no one else has." He shook his head to reinforce his answer. The tips of Anna's fingers tingled.

"What about the back door leading from the apartment directly to the inside of the garage?" A muscle twitched in Eli's jaw.

"No one uses that door." Tom pulled a rag out of his back pocket and wiped his hands.

"Are you afraid of something, Tom?" Eli crossed his arms and stepped toward the man.

Tom's eyes grew wide. "Of course I'm not afraid of anything. I have it pretty good around here. Living in grandpa's house. I don't need any trouble from you."

"We're not looking to cause trouble."

Tom nodded. There was something about him. He seemed…fearful. "I got nothing to hide. I have a good job. Don't go stirring the pot."

Eli clapped Tom on the shoulder. "Okay, well, we'll lock up when we leave. You'll let me know if anyone else comes around?"

Tom nodded again. "Grab Daniel's stuff while you're here. My aunt Beth has been on the warpath. She wants it all gone."

"We know, the sheriff told us."

"Sorry about that." Tom looked genuinely contrite. "The Christophers are used to getting their way." A gruff laugh escaped his lips. "I don't want to give her a reason to kick me to the curb. I like my job."

Anna swallowed a lump in her throat. "We've had a lot going on. Give me a few days and I'll get his stuff." Her gaze traveled to the staircase. "The furniture came with the apartment?"

"Yes, most of it anyway. You have to remove his personal stuff. You know, his clothes in the drawers and maybe throw out whatever you don't want. I'd feel bad going through his stuff. Your brother was a good guy." Tom frowned, as if giving it thoughtful consideration. "I mean, the few times I saw him."

"I'll do that. Do you know where I can get some boxes?"

Tom's face brightened, as if he were eager to please. "There are some in the basement." He turned and started toward the house. "I'll get them for you."

Eli and Anna climbed the steps to the garage apartment. Now that the initial shock of her brother's death had worn off, she was struck by how sparse his living conditions had been. One of the few personal items he had was the framed photo of the two of them. This time she picked it up and dropped it into her purse. She pushed a strand of hair behind her ears. "I wish I hadn't lost contact with Daniel. Maybe things would be different now."

Eli searched each drawer of the desk. "Don't beat yourself up."

Anna nodded. If anyone understood regrets, it was Eli.

He closed the last drawer. "Where did you see the lighter?"

"Over there." She pointed to the end table next to the couch. All but one cushion was still on the floor. She recognized the table as one that used to sit in their childhood family room. It had seemed out of place even then in her parents' perfectly maintained home. She ran her fingers along the edge. "The lighter was sitting on this table. My mom always kept it next to the couch." She clenched her hands. "One of her vices. Besides my father." She bit out the last words.

Her eyes dropped to the lip of the table. The marble top was removable. Anna and Daniel used to hide papers and tiny items in the small space between the marble and the wood frame. She removed the lamp from the table and set it on the floor. Wedging her small fingers between the marble and wood, she worked it up. Eli slipped in next to her and lifted the heavy marble.

White fabric in a plastic bag stood out in stark contrast to the dark maple wood. White dots danced in her line of vision. Glancing over her shoulder, she found Eli staring in disbelief. Sliding in next to her, he scooped up the bag and turned it over in his hands. Moving as if in a trance, he dropped down on to the couch. The cushion released a spray of dust that hung in the stream of sunlight shining in through dirty windows. Anna dropped to her knees in front of him and slid her hands under his. "Mary's bonnet?"

He nodded. Through the bag he thumbed the pale gray stitching against the white garment. "She was learning to sew." A muscle in his jaw twitched. The rims of his eyes grew red.

A buzzing started in her head. "How did it get in there?"

Eli took Anna's hands in his, moved her aside and stood up. She narrowed her gaze, trying to read his emotions. He paced the small space. "Daniel must have found her *kapp* and didn't know how to come forward with it. He had to know the initials embroidered on it stood for Mary Miller. But why didn't he show it to me when I met him?" His hands curled into fists.

"Maybe he was afraid he'd look guilty. Remember how paranoid he was? He wanted time to figure out who hurt Mary." It was the only thing that made sense right from the beginning.

Eli plowed a hand through his hair and stopped pacing, turning to face Anna. "Let's go pay another visit to Tiffany. Maybe she's up for talking longer. Maybe Daniel confided in her after all."

"Wait." Anna held out her hand. "Are you okay?"

Eli glanced down at the *kapp.* He couldn't believe he held

it in his hand. He remembered the day Mary had proudly sewn the string back on after she tore it climbing the back fence. His chest tightened. "This is the first solid clue I've had in Mary's disappearance."

"Do you think my brother had something to do with it?"

The pleading look in her eyes toyed with his rioting emotions. "Sit down." Tears gathered in the corners of her eyes as she sat down on the couch and he sat on the corner of the coffee table. Their knees brushed briefly before she angled them away.

"I don't know."

A tear escaped and slid down her cheek. Anna's shoulders visibly sagged. She lowered her eyes, her long lashes brushing against her fair skin. He struggled to catch a decent breath. Reaching out, he captured her hands when it looked like she wanted to flee. "Hear me out." Her eyes grew hard and locked with his, challenging him. "Your brother knew *something*. I don't know if he uncovered it because of the photos he was taking. Perhaps he stumbled onto something and didn't know who to trust. It's obvious the sheriff is protective of the Christopher family. And his own son."

Anna pulled her hands out of his grasp and crossed her arms over her chest. Her thin frame shuddered. "Or—" he ran a hand across his jaw, regretting the pain he was causing her "—he had firsthand knowledge of what happened to my sister and he came back to Apple Creek to set things right. He wanted to make sure he rounded up all the players so everyone involved would be punished." He held out Mary's *kapp*. *Poor sweet Mary*. "I can't figure out how he found this in the first place."

All the color drained from Anna's face. "You're right, we should talk to Tiffany again."

Eli glanced down at the *kapp* and ran his hand across

the plastic bag protecting it. "I should probably contact my office, let them know what we have."

"What about the sheriff?"

Eli knew Anna didn't like the sheriff any more than he did.

He thought of Abram and Mariam, whose hearts would be torn anew when they learned what they had found. He ran a hand across the back of his neck. Wasn't this what he had worked for all these years? Too many unanswered questions remained. He wanted to be the one to tell his parents.

He stood and offered his hand to Anna. "The sheriff can wait. Let's talk to Tiffany."

Before they reached the hospital, Eli called his contact at the hospital to make sure Tiffany didn't have any visitors. Even with the reassurance she was alone, Anna's nerve endings hummed to life. The last thing she wanted was a run-in with someone from the Christopher family.

Tiffany's condition had improved, so she had been moved out of ICU. When they reached her room, they found her sitting up in bed chatting on her cell phone. When Tiffany noticed them, she froze. "I have to go," she said into the phone, then pulled it away from her ear. She held the cell phone between her palms and stared at them.

"Hi, Tiffany." Anna stood tentatively in the doorway. Tiffany waved, the beginning of a smile on her pale lips. "How are you feeling?"

The young girl raised her bandaged arm. "Besides my broken arm and leg? I'll survive. I think they're sending me home soon, but I'm going to require help getting around."

"I imagine your family—"

Tiffany waved her hand, cutting her off. "My family can afford to hire a nurse to help me. They don't want anything to cut into their lunch and shopping time."

Anna suddenly felt sorry for Tiffany. She wanted to re-assure her that her parents cared, then she thought of her own parents. Her mother cared, but not enough to get her-self and her family out of harm's way. Something pinged her conscience. Was it really fair to blame her mother? Her father had a hold on her. She had been trapped.

"We wanted to talk to you again about your time with Daniel," Eli said.

Tiffany looked up, tears welling in her blue eyes. "I don't know what to tell you."

"You said Daniel was fascinated with the Mary Miller case. What *exactly* did he say?" Anna wrapped her hands around the cool metal of the bedside rail.

Tiffany stopped fingering the edge of her bedspread and glanced over, meeting Anna's gaze. "Why?" She lowered her voice. "Did he actually find something?"

"What was he looking for, Tiffany?" Eli asked. "Don't let his death be in vain."

Tiffany's eyes widened. "What do you mean?" Her brows furrowed. "You're scaring me."

Eli looked at Anna, as if asking for permission. "We have reason to believe the plane was sabotaged."

The color of Tiffany's face matched the crisp white hos-pital linens. With a shaky hand she clutched the sheet to her chest. "I was on that plane." Her eyes moved rapidly, as if she was remembering something. "In the final minutes he was scrambling to keep it in the air. He was rambling that someone messed with the plane. He was in a panic."

Anna's gut tightened. "Did Daniel ever tell you he sus-pected someone was out to get him?" She hated to ask, knowing it made her brother sound unstable.

Tiffany pulled her hair back off her face but didn't say anything.

"Please, Tiffany, if you know anything…" Anna urged.

Tiffany worked her bottom lip. "Daniel told me he thought my brother and a few other guys at the fraternity had something to do with the little Amish girl's disappearance." The way she referred to Mary seemed impersonal. Tiffany must have realized it because her attention darted toward the door, then to Eli. "He was obsessed with your sister's disappearance."

"What made him suspect his fraternity brothers?" Eli's voice sounded even, unaffected.

"He heard them arguing the night your sister went missing."

"You didn't believe him?" Anna's knees grew weak. She dropped into the vinyl chair next to the bed. Eli touched her shoulder.

Tiffany shrugged. "I didn't. I'm sorry I didn't tell you everything before. My brother can be a jerk...but hurt a child?" She brushed a tear from her cheek. "Chase has two young boys of his own. I didn't want to cause trouble for him. Some of Daniel's ideas seemed so out there."

"Did he tell you what he overheard?" Eli squeezed Anna's shoulder.

"After the guys in the fraternity argued, he said they went up to my grandfather's cabin. Daniel didn't go with them." She twisted her lips. "Daniel was obsessed with searching the place, but if he found anything he never told me." Her brow furrowed. She lowered her voice. "*Did* he find something?"

Eli and Anna locked gazes. Anna leaned forward and touched Tiffany's hand, but Eli was the first to speak. "For your own protection, I don't want to tell you anything more than you already know. Do you still have my business card?" Tiffany nodded slowly. "Don't tell your family we were here. But if you hear anything else, will you let me know?"

Fear etched lines around Tiffany's eyes. "Did Chase hurt your little sister?"

"I don't know."

"Will you find out?" Tiffany asked, a hard set to her pale blue eyes. "My mother always made excuses for him. If he was involved, maybe once in his life, he'll have to take responsibility for it."

Eli nodded. "Rest. Call me if you need anything."

As they walked down the hospital corridor, Anna turned to Eli. "How do we prove Chase was involved?"

"We still need to connect the pieces. It's a long shot, but I'm going to send Mary's *kapp* to FBI forensics. Maybe they can get some DNA from it. Meanwhile, I can track down the fraternity brothers. If they know we found evidence, maybe one of them will crack. It's only a theory. But it's the best one we have."

Eli reached out and took Anna's hand. Her heart went out to him. "There's one more thing."

Her limbs suddenly felt heavy. "What?"

"You need to leave Apple Creek."

"I want to help you. Clear my brother's name. And I still have to clean out his things from the apartment."

The fight was draining from her. They had argued about this a million times before, it seemed. She dragged a hand through her hair. "Maybe it's time I went home and put my brother to rest. Maybe this will give me some sense of peace so I can return later and deal with his things." She looked up and met his gaze. "Promise me you'll be fair, no matter what you discover."

"I promise." He squeezed her hand. "Thank you."

Eli sat at his parents' kitchen table while Mariam stood at the sink nervously wringing her hands. She obviously sensed this visit was like no other. Samuel had been sent out to the field to get their father. Katie Mae sat across from him while Anna went upstairs to pack her things. Because Mary's *kapp* had been found in Daniel's possession, Anna claimed she wasn't comfortable joining them when he broke the news.

A cold knot fisted his gut. The only moment Eli dreaded more than this one was when he had to face his parents for the first time after Mary's disappearance. He exhaled sharply and bowed his head. *God please give me the words to tell my parents.*

A quiet calm settled over him. He opened his eyes and looked around the neat space. His parents were God fearing. They didn't deserve any of this. *Who did?*

"What's this about?" Mariam asked for the second time since they had arrived. She leaned against the stove and fiddled with the folds in her apron.

Eli stood and reached for his mother's hand. She took it tentatively and he guided her to a seat. "Let's wait for *Dat.*"

Mariam's gaze drifted to Mary's empty seat. She ran her fingers along the smooth pine of the long table, her eyes filling with worry. He'd do anything to take this pain from his mother.

Heavy footsteps sounded on the back porch. In unison, everyone's attention swung to the back door. First Samuel appeared in the doorway. He hung his hat on the hook then walked over and stood by the counter. He seemed reluctant to sit down. Then his father strode through the door. Abram's eyes grew wide, then he seemed to catch himself. He slowed, taking in the scene in front of him.

It was Mariam who spoke first. "Sit, Abram. Eli has news."

Abram wore a mask of stone. He took off his hat and hung it next to Samuel's on the hook by the door. He strolled over to where they had gathered and pulled out his seat, the chair legs scrapping across the floor. Everything seemed to play out in slow motion.

When his father finally sat, Eli slipped the clear plastic bag with Mary's *kapp* from Anna's bag resting against his chair. He pushed it toward his father and mother. A quiet gasp escaped his mother's lips. She pressed a trembling hand to her mouth. The hurt in his mother's eyes tore at his heart.

His father's lower lip quivered. He reached out and ran a wrinkled hand across the bag. "It is a child's *kapp*." His voice lifted in a slight lilt, but there was no doubt in his eyes.

Eli nodded. "We found it today."

"It's Mary's." His mother's words came out in a painful sob. Tears burned the back of Eli's eyes. "And Mary?" The hope in his mother's face was too much to bear. "Did you find our sweet Mary?"

Eli struggled to find the right words. "I didn't find Mary."

Abram pushed back and stood. He slapped his palm on the table, his body shaking with rage. "Why do you bring this here and say it's Mary's? It could be any child's."

Mariam reached for the bag and pulled it toward her. "It is Mary's." Through the bag she traced the ragged gray stitching his little sister had taken great care with. And the initials his sister had stitched.

Abram picked up the chair and slammed the four legs down with one loud thud. "We must have faith in God. It is a fool's errand to keep after this ten years later. We must forgive and move on." Fear blended with his anger.

Katie Mae found her voice, albeit soft and tremulous. "Where did you find this?"

Eli stared at the white garment. "In Daniel Quinn's apartment."

"Anna's brother hurt our Mary?" Katie Mae's voice rose into a near screech. "Daniel was here. On our farm. Taking photographs." Covering her face with her hands, she crumpled into soft sobs.

"I'm trying to figure it out." Eli glanced toward the kitchen door, wondering if Anna could hear the conversation. "Anna is upstairs packing her things. I've arranged for Dominic to take her home. It will be better for everyone."

Mariam folded her hands on top of the table. "We must have forgiveness in our hearts. We cannot blame her for her brother's actions. She is hurting now." The Amish's ability to forgive was remarkable.

"*Mem,* she needs to go." Eli rose and turned to find Anna standing in the doorway with her suitcase in hand. Pink rimmed her hazel eyes.

Katie Mae stood and approached Anna, her hands twisted in the folds of her dress. "I forgive your brother."

Anna's eyes grew wide and filled with tears. Her mouth opened, then snapped shut. Her knuckles whitened on the handle of the suitcase. "I'm sorry about Mary. But I don't believe my brother did this. I think he was trying to help solve the case because he suspected—"

Eli gave her a curt nod, indicating he didn't want her to say anymore.

Anna covered her mouth. "I am so sorry for your loss."

Mariam sat at the table and nodded, a single tear trailing down her cheek. Abram stood silently in the corner. Both of his parents seemed transfixed by the child's *kapp* in the center of the table.

Anna crossed the kitchen and stopped by the door, her back to them. Her shoulders rose and fell, her chestnut brown curls flowing down her back. Slowly, she turned around. "I know my brother could have never hurt your child." She hiked her chin and drew in a shuddering breath. "I will keep you all in my prayers."

She turned and left. The screen door closed with a resounding thwack. Eli forced himself to stay seated for a moment longer, knowing Dominic would keep her safe until he could go to her. For now, he had to be here for his family.

Anna stepped onto the porch, and the cool evening air hit her fiery cheeks. The whisper of doubt regarding her brother was going to kill her. How could she move forward if they never found the truth? Yet she knew Eli was right. She had to leave town for now. She took some consolation in knowing she'd return to her high school students. Her mind needed the distraction.

And finally, she could inter Daniel's ashes next to their mother's. She bit her lower lip and pushed the thought aside.

Filling her lungs with the fresh country air, she crossed the yard. She'd miss this place. Dominic opened the back door of his black SUV and Anna tossed her bag in. Her car was still at the shop getting the window replaced. She figured the car was ready, but Eli insisted she ride with— she flicked a glance at her chauffeur's bulging biceps—the Hulk. Eli said he'd have someone drop her car off at her house in Buffalo in a few days. She held on to the small hope that *someone* would be Eli.

As she walked around to the passenger side, she heard Eli calling her name. She turned to see him jogging down the steps and across the lawn. Her mood buoyed.

Dominic climbed into the car and closed the door, presumably to give them privacy. Eli took Anna's hands in his. "I'll keep you posted."

Pursing her lips, she nodded. "I hope you find the truth. I need to know my brother's innocent."

Eli squeezed her hands but didn't say anything. Not exactly a ringing endorsement for her brother's innocence. "It was great to meet you. I wish it had been under better circumstances." His words seemed stilted.

"Is this goodbye?"

"I want to know you're safe. I know Dominic will take care of you while I investigate things here."

Anna's gaze drifted to the cornfields behind him. Much of the corn had been harvested for feed. The scent of earth filled her nose. Finally finding her nerve, she leaned in and brushed a kiss across his smooth cheek. He smelled of soap and aftershave. "Goodbye, Eli," she whispered in his ear.

He swept his thumb across the back of her hand. "Goodbye, Anna."

FIFTEEN

With an unfocused gaze, Anna stared over the fields as Dominic pulled onto the road. Gently, with the pad of her finger, she traced the spot where Eli's whiskers had brushed her face. If only they had met at a different time, under different circumstances, she might have finally been willing to let down her guard. To give someone a chance. Even someone in law enforcement. But as long as there was an inkling in Eli's mind that her brother was guilty of hurting his sister, they'd never have a future.

The SUV crested the hill and eventually fields gave way to more frequent houses. Anna glanced at Dominic. He stared straight ahead. Unfortunately he wasn't the chatty type. She could have used the distraction.

As they approached the center of Apple Creek, her cell phone rang. She pulled it out of her purse. Her brows furrowed. "Hello."

The man on the other end of the phone cleared his throat. "Yeah, Anna. It's Tom Hanson."

"Hi, Tom." She sensed his apprehension. "Is something wrong?"

"I hate to do this to you, but my aunt Beth, uh, Mrs. Christopher, is determined to get rid of your brother's things. She told me to put it all out by the curb tonight."

A pounding started in the back of her head. A long pause floated across the line. "And tomorrow's garbage pickup."

Looking out the window, she realized they were driving farther out of town. A warning voice whispered in her head. *Don't lose what little connection you have to your big brother.* "Any chance you can put the stuff in a corner of the garage for now?" She cut a sideways glance at Dominic. "I'm busy now."

"My aunt's pretty mad. I don't want to lose my job over this."

Anna worked her bottom lip. She sensed Dominic looking at her. "What's wrong?" His deep voice startled her.

"Hold on," she said into the phone. Turning to Dominic she said, "The Christophers are going to throw my brother's things out."

"Tell him to store them. Eli wants you out of Apple Creek." *Eli wants you out...* Dominic's words hurt more than they should have.

"Please, it will only take a minute." She thought about her grandmother's end table, and her brother's photographs were like a window into his soul. What Mrs. Christopher considered junk were the only things she had left from her family.

When Dominic didn't say anything, Anna put the phone back to her ear. "I'm not far. I'll be there in a few minutes. Can you meet me at his apartment?"

"I'm here now. See you in a few."

Anna tossed the phone into her purse. "Dominic, we need to make a quick detour."

"No way. Eli told me to get you out of Apple Creek."

"It will take five minutes. My brother's apartment is just down the road. Turn around, please."

Dominic huffed and slapped the steering wheel. When

he slowed the vehicle and did a three-point turn in the middle of the road, Anna's shoulders sagged. "Thank you."

They drove back through Apple Creek toward Daniel's garage apartment. She pointed to the house. "Turn in here." The sun had set and long shadows gathered in the corners of the long driveway. "Pull around back and park near the steps. It should only take a few minutes to load up. Tom says he already put things in boxes."

Dominic threw the gear into park. "If Eli gets wind of this, he'll have my head."

"He won't ever know," she said conspiratorially.

Dominic muttered under his breath, then pointed to the steps hugging one side of the garage. "Your brother's apartment is up there?"

"Yes."

"Okay." Her bodyguard turned and glared at her. "You stay put. Stay inside the vehicle. Give me your cell phone." She handed him her phone and he punched in a few numbers, programming his number directly into her cell. "Call me if you see anyone. Got it?"

Anna swallowed hard. Icy fear pricked her skin. All they were doing was picking up her brother's things. So why did she suddenly feel like they were on a covert mission?

Tom appeared at the bottom of the steps. He waved them over. "You hear me?" Dominic said in a commanding voice. "Stay put. I'll get your brother's things."

Dominic climbed out of the vehicle, then paused in the open doorway. "Take the keys. Just in case."

Anna's mouth grew dry. They were picking up a few things, she reminded herself. *Just getting a few things.* She hoped he remembered the end table and the framed photos. Leaning back against the cool leather of the seat, she tried to relax.

She watched as Dominic followed Tom up the steps.

From her vantage point she could see them enter the apartment. A moment later, Dominic came out and put a box on the landing. He went back into the apartment. Anna tapped her fingers on the armrest of her door. She glanced down at her cell phone. Nervousness raked across her flesh when time seemed to stretch with no sign of Dominic or Tom.

She leaned forward. *Where are you?* Her fingers brushed against the handle, but Dominic's stern warning whispered across her brain. *Stay put.* She stared at her cell phone and waited ten minutes before dialing Dominic's phone number. No answer.

Her heart jackhammered. She glanced down at the keys in her hand. She could leave and go get Eli, but what about Dominic? She suddenly felt foolish. Dominic was probably helping Tom move something and couldn't get to his phone. She waited a few more minutes then dialed his number again. Still no answer.

A whisper of dread made the fine hairs on the back of her neck stand at attention. She shook the phone in her hand, willing it to ring. Maybe she should call Eli. And tell him what? That she convinced Dominic to ignore his instructions? A new wave of apprehension washed over her. Even if she wanted to call Eli, he didn't have cell phone reception at his parents' home.

Despite the fluttering in her chest, she unlocked the passenger door and pulled the handle. The dome light snapped on, bathing her in stark white light. She tried to shake the fear pulsing through her veins. She slipped out of the car and closed the door with a quiet click.

The deep hum of something mechanized made her pause. The garage door rumbled open. A mixture of relief and apprehension twined up her spine. Maybe they had used the back entry to carry some stuff out through the garage. Anna walked around to the back of Dominic's vehicle to pop the rear hatch. She was already out of the vehicle so she might as well help.

Soft steps crunched on the gravel driveway. She spun around to see Mrs. Christopher standing there with a sour expression on her face. Anna pressed a hand to her chest. "Oh, my goodness, you scared me. I'm picking up Daniel's things right now. We'll be out of your way shortly." She hated the breathless quality of her voice.

Mrs. Christopher narrowed her gaze. "Come with me."

Anna moved back around to the passenger door of Dominic's vehicle, suddenly wishing she had taken his advice and stayed safely inside.

"No, over here." Mrs. Christopher jaw clenched as she tilted her head toward the garage.

"I don't understand. A friend of mine is helping Tom bring my brother's things down." She glanced toward the steps, willing Dominic to appear.

That's when Anna saw the black object in Mrs. Christopher's hand. Anna's heart plummeted to her shoes. She blinked in confusion as she tried to process everything.

"Walk."

"Where...?"

Mrs. Christopher jammed the gun against Anna's rib cage. "The garage. Go."

Anna's gaze shifted to the stairs.

"No one is coming to help you," the older woman said. "Get in the driver's side."

Anna's eyes slid across the fancy sports car. "You want me to drive?"

Mrs. Christopher seemed mildly amused. "I can't very well drive and keep an eye on you." The way she waved the gun around made Anna wince. "Get in. I don't have time for this nonsense."

Anna did as she was told. She climbed into the driver's

seat and her knees hit the steering wheel. Out of the corner of her eye, she watched Mrs. Christopher walk around the back of the car. She took that moment to slip her cell phone out, dial 9-1-1 and hide it under the front seat. Her heart beat wildly in her ears when Mrs. Christopher got in the passenger's side.

"What were you doing?" The older woman's blue eyes flashed rage.

Anna's panicked thoughts mercifully tended toward survival. "I needed to adjust the seat. My knees...." She lifted her knee to bang against the steering wheel.

Silence stretched between them. Anna clenched her jaw. Mrs. Christopher leaned forward, keeping the gun trained on Anna. *Please don't let her find my phone.* As if an answer to her prayer, Mrs. Christopher leaned back. "It's the button on the side."

Anna reached down with her left hand and found a few buttons. She raised, lowered and moved her seat, pretending to be clueless, but she really was buying time. Hoping Dominic would suddenly appear.

"Hurry. It's time to go."

Not wanting to tempt fate, Anna pushed a button to start the car. Gripping the gear stick, she put it in drive and drove out of the garage.

"Drive and don't do anything stupid or—" she jerked her thumb toward the trunk "—you're not the only one whose life is at stake."

A horrible realization took hold. Had she somehow overpowered Dominic? As unreasonable as that seemed, a mental image of Dominic stuffed in the trunk came to mind. As she eased the car forward, she glanced around for Tom. No sign of him, either.

Her eyes dropped to the gun. With regret, Anna realized

even if this crazy person was a bad shot, she had a pretty good chance of hitting her in this small space.

"Where are you taking me?"

"To get the answers you've been dying to get."

SIXTEEN

"I'm taking you to the cabin. That's where the problem began…and ends." Mrs. Christopher sniffed.

"I don't understand. Why me?" Anna tracked the gun out of the corner of her eye.

"It didn't have to be this way. If only your brother had left well enough alone."

"My brother's dead. I bet you messed with his plane."

Mrs. Christopher chuckled, low and slightly amused. "You highly overestimate my willingness to get my hands dirty. But, yes, I did arrange it. Once I learned he had photographs, I had to find them. And you and your boyfriend just wouldn't quit."

"You won't get away with this. Eli will find you." *Please, Lord, let Eli find me in time.* She prayed the sheriff's office was tracking her 9-1-1 call on her cell phone neatly tucked under her seat. She only wished she had the time to tell the dispatcher her emergency. *Please, please, please let them investigate the call.*

Mrs. Christopher lowered the gun slightly and laughed. "No, he'll be coming after Tom Hanson. Not me. I'm a well-respected member of Apple Creek." She covered her mouth in mock surprise. "Your bodyguard never saw me. He didn't know what hit him. And, oh, dear, someone stole my car. Tom—the black sheep of the family—never could be trusted."

Mrs. Christopher sat up straighter in her seat. "Here, turn here."

Anna slowed the vehicle and turned up the familiar narrow road leading to the cabin in the woods. The vehicle rocked over the deep ruts and Anna wondered if the sports car would make it without getting stuck. Her gaze shifted to the gun. She wished Mrs. Christopher would move her finger away from the trigger. One deep rut and it would all be over.

The large tree still blocked the road. Mrs. Christopher's face was shrouded in shadows, but Anna suspected she hadn't anticipated this obstacle. "Get out."

Anna did as she was told. A breeze rustled the leaves, sending a whisper of dread across her goose-pimpled skin. Her gaze cut to Mrs. Christopher climbing out the other side. A momentary thought flashed through her mind. *Run.* She glanced down at her sandals, realizing she had a better chance of getting shot than getting away.

Dear Lord, let Eli find me in time.

Mrs. Christopher came up behind her and jabbed her in the back. Anna's head bounced forward. "Stop stalling. Get moving."

Moonlight poked through the branches. *Maybe I should run.* The gravel crunched under their unsteady steps. Mrs. Christopher wrapped her thin fingers more tightly around Anna's forearm, as if reading her mind.

"What happened to Mary?" If this was it, Anna wanted answers.

"What are you talking about?" Mrs. Christopher squared her shoulders, seemingly indignant.

"That's what this is all about, right? Something happened to Mary and the Christopher family wanted to pin it on my brother." It was the most logical conclusion.

"My son Chase has been in trouble since the day he was born." She pushed Anna forward again. "It only got worse after his father left."

Anna's mouth grew dry. "His father? I thought you and Mr. Christopher were still married."

"Yes. Chase is my husband's stepson."

"But they share the same last name?" Her mind whirred with the possibilities. A mosquito bit her cheek and she swatted at it.

"Richard would never adopt Chase, but he didn't argue when I legally changed my son's name to his. The Christopher name opens doors." In the dark, Anna imagined her captor hiking her proud chin. "Despite growing up in a privileged home, Chase tried to slam every single door shut. If my husband knew half the things Chase was involved with, he would have dumped him—dumped me—a long time ago." She stopped and turned, leaning close to Anna's face. A craziness lit her eyes. "I worked hard to get to this station in life. To have *everything* I could possibly want. I'm not going to let some ungrateful kid of mine ruin it for me. Or some nosy do-gooders."

Arching an eyebrow, Mrs. Christopher twisted her lips. "It's a shame really. Chase is a brilliant boy. He just doesn't think things through. I thought if Daniel's apartment was cleaned out, you'd have no reason to stay. I wanted you out of our lives."

Anna tried to take a step back, but Mrs. Christopher dug her thin fingers into her arm.

"Keep walking." The woman's energy level seemed to ramp up when the dark shadow of the cabin ruins came into view. The scent of charred wood reached Anna's nose and the memory of the inferno made her palms slick with sweat. Mrs. Christopher trudged past the cabin toward the tree where Daniel had taken photos of the bonnet. A dreadful thought whispered across her brain. *Does Mrs. Christopher know where Mary's body is buried?*

Instinctively Anna slowed her pace, and once again, Mrs. Christopher pushed her forward. "Come on." They reached a clearing. The ground dropped off and the lake stretched out in front of them. The moonlight glinted off the ripples. A soft breeze lifted the hair away from the clammy skin of her neck.

Dear Lord, please protect me.

Mrs. Christopher gestured with her gun down to the water. "You want to know what happened to Mary. You can join her."

Eli parked his SUV behind a sports car on the rutted road leading to the cabin. He had no idea what to expect when he drove out here. The dispatcher had told the sheriff about a dropped call from Anna's phone. The sheriff didn't waste any time contacting Eli. When Eli couldn't reach Anna or Dominic, he pulled some strings at his home FBI office to track the GPS on her phone. The signal was coming from right around here. He aimed the beam of the flashlight into the vehicle. It was empty. He'd have to call the plates in, but for now, he had to find Anna.

A thumping noise rattled the trunk. His pulse spiked. *Anna.* He yanked open the door and leaned into the backseat, feeling along its top for a lever. The seat flopped forward. He flashed the beam of his flashlight and froze when he found Tom Hanson lying on his back with his mouth, feet and hands bound. Eli ripped the silver duct tape from the startled man's face.

"Give me your hands," Eli commanded. Tom pushed his

bound hands through the opening. He cut the ropes with his pocketknife. "Can you pull yourself through?"

Groaning, Tom grabbed hold of the folded seat and pulled. Eli grasped his forearms and backed out of the car. After some awkward rearranging, Tom climbed out and sat on the front seat, his bound feet dangling out of the car.

"Where's Anna?" Eli squinted in the direction of the cabin but couldn't see past the tree cutting off the road. He bent over and cut the last of the ropes from Tom's ankles.

"That woman is crazy," Tom said. "She tricked me."

Eli glared at Tom. "What woman?"

"Aunt Beth. She's absolutely crazy. She promised me if I took care of things, I wouldn't have to be her lackey anymore." A sheen of sweat glistened on Tom's forehead.

"What things?" A knot formed in Eli's chest.

"I had to protect Chase." Tom scratched his head with reckless abandon.

"Which meant stopping Daniel from revealing what he found."

Tom rubbed his wrists where the ropes had dug into his flesh. "I only meant to scare Daniel. I didn't want anyone to die."

"So you sabotaged his plane?" Eli asked in disbelief.

"Yeah, well...."

"How did you think he'd survive a plane crash?"

"I didn't think. I just did what my aunt told me to do. She nearly went over the edge when she learned Tiffany had been in the plane. She wasn't supposed to be with Daniel that day." Tom glanced up at him with a contrite look on his face. "In the end, she got so desperate she had me wear an Amish hat while I set the cabin fire and plant the lighter to make it look like Anna was trying to destroy evidence."

Eli wanted to throttle this simpleton but realized now was not the time. "I need to find Anna *now*. Where is she?"

"Aunt Beth showed up at Daniel's apartment. The big guy—"

"Dominic?"

"Yeah, I guess. He was with Anna." Tom rubbed his wrists. "The big guy came up to the apartment to pick up Daniel's stuff. *She* wanted it gone." He raised an eyebrow. "But now I think she wanted to lure Anna there." His jaw worked. "My aunt had become unraveled. She snuck up behind Dominic and bashed him over the head with her gun. He went down in a heap." He curled his nose. "Never seen a big guy go down so hard. I don't think he's dead, but he's going to have a whopper of a headache." He scratched his head and winced. "I can relate."

Eli ran a hand across his mouth, his patience evaporating. "Where *is* Anna?"

"I don't know. My aunt asked me to come down into the garage through the back stairway. You know the one that leads directly into the garage? When I got down to the garage, she had her trunk open. Next thing I know, she *bashed* me." He rubbed his head. "Lights out." He lifted his palms. "And here I am."

Eli pointed at Tom. "Stay here. I'll deal with you later." He turned and jogged toward the cabin.

Dear Lord, guide me. Let me save Anna.

A stiff wind gusted off the lake, nearly drowning Mrs. Christopher's words.

"Why did you hurt Mary?" Anna asked, her voice shaking.

"My son—" the older woman's lips thinned as if she were holding back her temper "—is not a strong man. I blame myself. I always catered to him." The moonlight glinted in the whites of her eyes.

Something by the tree line caught Anna's attention. She

captured Eli's gaze and held it. Her legs almost went out from under her. *Thank you, God.* Eli held a finger to his lips.

"One night, Chase and a bunch of his fraternity brothers were drinking. The Blakely boy had borrowed a Taser from his father's trunk. He's the sheriff's son, you know. All they meant to do was have a little fun. Show off. Maybe scare the horse a little. All the other guys went into a bar and Chase… I don't think he even touched the animal. Just activated the Taser in front of the horse's nose.

"He didn't know the Amish girl was in the buggy." Mrs. Christopher's gaze grew vacant. "Chase said she didn't make a sound. He saw her head pop up at the last minute and she looked at him with wide eyes. She saw Chase."

"The child had a name. Mary Miller," Anna said through clenched teeth.

Mrs. Christopher seemed to consider this for only a moment. "Chase called me, blubbering. He was always calling me, looking for me to solve his problems. He had followed the buggy in his car. When the buggy crashed, the Amish girl tumbled out. Chase put her in the car and I told him to meet me here. He was completely panicked. She must have hit her head because she wasn't breathing by the time I got to her. I told him not to tell anybody." Mrs. Christopher ran a finger along her lower lip, as if reliving the night. "When I got here, I sent my son away."

"What did you do?" Anna's eyes grew wide with the realization, keenly aware of Eli listening from a few feet away.

"It was perfect." She ignored her question, as if fascinated by her own story. "As long as everyone kept quiet, no one ever had to know. We could go on living as we were accustomed." A quiet sob fell from her lips, the first sign of any remorse. "Your brother didn't need to get involved.

He wasn't even there that night. But he suspected something. I think he overheard his fraternity brothers arguing. He couldn't leave well enough alone.

"I had to do it. It was the only way to protect my son. To protect me." The proud woman's jaw was set in determination. "I threw Mary's body off this cliff. Her stupid bonnet got hung up on a branch. I was afraid if I threw it after her, it would float on the surface. So I stuffed it under a floorboard in the cabin. I should have buried it somewhere, but the ground was too hard. I didn't have any tools," she muttered, as if realizing the one mistake that had unraveled all her plans.

Mrs. Christopher gave her head a curt nod, as if snapping out of her reverie. She trained the gun on Anna's chest. "Now it's your turn."

In a flash, Mrs. Christopher dropped to the ground. A primal cry rang out from the otherwise dignified woman. Anna backed away from the edge, her legs crumbling underneath her. Anna knelt on the ground as Eli pulled Mrs. Christopher's arms behind her back and put on handcuffs. He dragged her to a seated position away from the ledge. He grabbed her gun and tucked it into his waistband.

Under the moonlight, Mrs. Christopher's face grew hard. She glared at Anna. "You ruined everything."

"Thank God you found me." Her heart filled with joy.

Eli cupped her cheeks and pressed his lips against her forehead. "I tracked the GPS on your phone. Smart girl."

Eli stood and pulled Anna up with him. She buried her face into his solid chest. "I've never been happier to see anyone in my entire life," she said.

He brushed his finger across her cheek. "Me, neither."

Mrs. Christopher rocked back and forth and moaned something unintelligible.

"I am so sorry about Mary," Anna said.

"Me, too." Eli tucked a strand of hair behind her ear and a slow smile spread across his face. "Thank God you're safe. Are you okay to walk on your own?"

"Yes," Anna whispered. "Do what you have to do with her."

Eli leaned over and grabbed the woman by her arm, bringing her to her feet. His features hardened. "Come on. We have some other people to track down."

"Leave my son out of this," Mrs. Christopher screeched at the top of her lungs. "It's Tom Hanson's fault. He's an idiot. He screwed everything up. If he had only followed my instructions exactly…"

The entire walk back to the car, Mrs. Christopher wailed and moaned. When they got closer to the road, the red and blue lights from the sheriff's cruiser lit the area. Tom Hanson was already in custody. Eli handed Mrs. Christopher to the sheriff.

"You need to send a unit over to Daniel Quinn's apartment right away. A friend of mine was knocked unconscious by Mrs. Christopher." Eli's stomach twisted and he sent up a silent prayer for Dominic.

Eli waited for the sheriff to finish his call, then said, "Thanks for not dismissing Anna's 9-1-1 call. You saved her life." He brushed a mosquito off his forearm. "Sheriff, we need to talk to your son about the night my sister disappeared."

The sheriff's brow furrowed. "Why?" Then his features softened. His shoulders sagged. "I will bring him in first thing in the morning."

"With your okay, I'd like to pick up Chase Christopher tonight."

The sheriff nodded.

Anna rested her hand on Eli's back and leaned into him.

Wrapping an arm around her shoulders, he pulled her closer. Her entire body relaxed. "Finally, justice for Mary," she whispered.

EPILOGUE

It felt good to be back in Apple Creek after a few weeks away. Most of the cornfields had been harvested, changing the appearance of the landscape. Slouching in the passenger seat of Eli's car, a million thoughts floated through her mind.

Eli had finally gotten the answers he had been looking for. Chase and Beth Christopher had been arrested for their roles in Mary's death. Tom Hanson was also in custody.

Eli had told her how Tom had owned up to sabotaging Daniel's plane and setting the cabin on fire with the hope of destroying any possible evidence against Chase. From his jail cell, Tom was spilling the rest of the family secrets. Under his aunt's instructions, he had been stalking Anna. He watched her from the barn loft, trailed her in the cornfield and nearly ran her over in town. Mrs. Christopher had hoped to chase Anna out of town, counting on Eli to pin Mary's disappearance on Anna's brother. In her eyes, Anna was the only one with a stake in proving Daniel's innocence. When Anna wouldn't leave, the threats escalated. A cold chill ran down her spine.

The sheriff's son had cooperated fully. He didn't have knowledge of the crime, but he had lied about Chase's alibi at the time Mary went missing. If only he hadn't been intimidated by the Christopher family all those years ago, the Miller family would have found the answers they needed.

And Anna had her answer, too. Daniel was innocent.

"How is your family doing?" she finally asked, breaking the silence.

"My parents' propensity for forgiveness is incredible. They are at peace."

"How is Dominic?"

"Mostly embarrassed. Mrs. Christopher had caught him with the butt of her gun from behind, knocking him out." Eli ran his palm along the steering wheel. "Thank God she didn't shoot him."

Anna glanced over at Eli. "How about you? Have you found peace?"

"I'm working on it. I've gone to a few church services over the past few weeks." Half of his mouth slanted into a wry grin. "I'm a work in progress."

"Good. Good." Anna wrapped her fingers around the smooth vinyl of the armrest between them.

"I'm sorry I wasn't there for your brother's service," Eli said, never taking his eyes off the road. "I had to be in court."

Anna waved her hand in dismissal. "I understand. I had his ashes buried next to my mother's. It felt good to have some closure. And your family had a service for Mary?" They never found Mary's body, but at least they found peace in having some answers.

Eli nodded. "Yes. Buggies lined up as far as the eye could see. It provided healing for all of us."

"And Samuel and Katie Mae? How are they?" She watched the trees rush by outside her passenger window, feeling like she was asking him twenty questions. But there were so many things she still wanted to know.

"Samuel is coming around. He's always been so quiet.

But he seems more content. I don't think my mother has to worry about him leaving. He seems committed to sticking around." He shrugged. "He's sweet on an Amish girl who lives on a neighboring farm. Time will tell.

"Katie Mae and Isaac officially announced their engagement."

Anna's eyes widened. "Really? Are you happy about that?"

Eli made a deep noise in his throat. "What do I know? I had a long conversation with Isaac recently. Maybe I judged him too harshly. He claimed he was abrasive with me because he feared I'd talk Katie Mae out of marrying him. It was a defense mechanism. He does seem to love her."

"You're turning into a softie." Anna patted his knee, then pulled her hand away. "How is Tiffany?"

"She's on the mend. She has a ways to go both physically and mentally. It's a lot to deal with, learning your brother and mother are capable of such evil. At least she has her father. Mr. Christopher knew nothing about the incident. He'd been too busy working and building his empire."

Eli turned his vehicle up the narrow road leading to the cabin. The search crews looking for Mary's body had cleared the tree from the road. They reached the burned-out cabin and Eli stopped the vehicle. They climbed out. Anna opened the back door and grabbed the bouquet of wildflowers.

Red lifted his head, seemingly content to rest on the backseat. Eli brushed past Anna and hooked Red's leash. "Come on." He patted the dog's head, and he jumped out of the car.

They followed a zigzag path to the clearing. Red sniffed everything in his path. Eli wrapped the leash tightly around his hand when they reached the cliff, and Anna leaned forward and glanced down to the chilly lake waters. Although the dive team had not been able to find Mary's remains, the Millers' strong faith gave them peace. It had been ten years, and they finally had answers. What they had always known was still true—their beloved daughter was in heaven.

"Would you like to say a prayer?" Anna asked.

Eli bowed his head, reached out and captured Anna's hand. "Dear Lord, thank You for letting me find justice for Mary. Please let all those hurt by the cruel acts of that day find peace." He squeezed her hand. "Thank You for the gift of Mary's life, however short."

A brisk wind whipped up across the lake and Anna pulled her coat tighter, the wildflowers brushing her nose. Eli wrapped his arm around her shoulder and held her close. Red sat down next to her feet. "And thank You, Lord, for bringing Anna into my life. I am truly thankful for my blessings. Amen."

Warmth blossomed in her chest. She handed Eli half of the bouquet and together they tossed them. The wildflowers rained down on to the surface of the lake. They watched in silence as the colorful flowers bobbed and dipped, floating out toward the horizon.

Eli turned Anna to face him, searching her face with intense eyes. "I don't want to lose you."

"I...don't..."

Eli touched his finger to her lips. A smile pulled on the corners of her mouth and joy filled her heart. "If you'll have me, Miss Anna Quinn, I'd like to court you." Her insides tingled.

She cupped his face with her hands and kissed his cheek. He grabbed her wrists in one of his and planted a firm kiss on her lips.

After a moment, he pulled away, a question in his eyes. Anna couldn't contain her smile.

"Can I take that as a yes?" Eli asked.

"Yes!" Anna threw her arms around his neck and squeezed. "I'd love for you to court me."

Red jumped up, resting one paw on Eli's thigh and the other on Anna's waist. Laughing, they both fluffed the Irish setter's ears. "You want in on this, too, huh?" Eli asked.

Red barked, then dropped down. Spinning in a tight circle, he settled back in at their feet.

Anna pressed her cheek to Eli's chest and he wrapped his strong arms tightly around her. The sweet scent of the crisp fall air filled her senses. She tried to memorize every detail of the glorious moment. *I am truly blessed.*

Eli pressed a kiss to the crown of her head. He leaned back and tucked a strand of hair behind her ear, leaving a trail of warmth under his touch. "Ready?"

She nodded. "Ready."

* * * * *

Dear Reader,

I am so excited to share *Plain Pursuit,* my first Love Inspired Suspense title, with you. It has been a dream of mine to write for Harlequin.

At the 2011 Romance Writers of America conference in New York City, I heard the Love Inspired Suspense line was looking for more Amish stories. I had long been fascinated with the Amish after seeing an Amish gentleman and his buggy while on a family vacation when I was a little girl. I couldn't fathom living without cars or electricity. What? No *Happy Days* or *Laverne and Shirley?*

I came home from the conference and decided this was the perfect opportunity to learn more about that community. I read memoirs of former Amish, nonfiction and lots of blogs. I even took my two young daughters on a ride to an Amish community sixty miles south of my home near Buffalo, New York. The yummy Amish-made chocolates were the highlight of the trip.

Through all my research, I learned the Amish lifestyle can differ from community to community. They live by a set of rules called the *Ordnung.* The rules cover things such as the style of buggy, the color of men's shirts or whether or not the homes can have upholstered furniture. The leaders can change the rules, but they must be endorsed by the community in a show of unity. *Plain Pursuit* is set in a fictional town called Apple Creek, New York, allowing me the freedom to capture the feel of an authentic Amish community without being beholden to any one "real" community.

I also learned the Amish have a strong propensity for forgiveness. This was never more evident than during the Nickel Mines, Pennsylvania, tragedy in 2006 when five young Amish girls were killed by a gunman. The idea of forgiveness is a running theme in *Plain Pursuit*. Eli is determined to find justice for his little sister, but he also must find forgiveness in his heart if he truly wants to find peace. Anna, too, must find peace after losing her brother in a plane crash.

I hope you enjoyed your visit to Apple Creek.

Live, Love, Laugh,

Alison Stone

Questions for Discussion

1. Jesus's parable of the servant who asked his master for forgiveness but then turned around and denied his fellow servant forgiveness (*Matthew* 18:21-35) is part of the Amish lectionary. The Amish believe firmly that they must forgive their fellow man if they want to be forgiven by God. Do you think if you were Eli, you could forgive the person who hurt your little sister?

2. Have you ever been cross with someone who hurt you? What happened when you made a decision to forgive them? Did you feel relieved? At peace?

3. Readers seem to be fascinated with the Amish lifestyle. Is there any aspect of their lifestyle that appeals to you?

4. If you had to give up technology, what would you miss most? Do you see any advantages to giving up technology?

5. Eli wasn't forthcoming in telling Anna her brother was under investigation. She only found out when the sheriff mentioned it after she opened her brother's apartment to him. Do you think it was wrong for Eli to keep this information from Anna?

6. Samuel, Mary's twin, lived with a lot of guilt over his sister's disappearance. The last time he spoke to her, he had teased her. Do you make a habit of always parting with loved ones on good terms?

7. Samuel needs to learn to forgive himself. Do you think it's harder to forgive yourself or someone else?

8. Do you think it's possible for Eli to find a new church home after leaving the Amish? Have you ever had to find a new church home? What made you feel welcome?

9. What happened to little Mary Miller that fateful night stayed shrouded in mystery in part because people were afraid to come forward. Have you ever been in a situation when it was difficult to come forward and tell the truth? What would you say to young people today about peer pressure?

10. Anna grew up in a violent home. When Anna was a young girl, her father cracked when he realized his family was going to leave. As a result, Anna lost both parents that day. How do you think Anna's life would have been different if her mother had decided to stay with her father?

11. The Amish have a practice of shunning a person who has gone against Amish beliefs. They shun the offender in part because they don't want him to be a bad example to the other members of the community and in the hopes the offender will mend his ways. We might call it "tough love." Eli was never truly shunned because he left the Amish before he was baptized; however, he never overstays his welcome because his father fears he'll be a negative influence, especially on his younger brother. Do you think this treatment is too harsh?

12. People respond differently to their circumstances. Eli's tragic past made him pull away from his faith,

whereas Anna relied on her faith to get her through her tragic past. Why do you think people have different reactions? Is your faith strong enough to sustain you through dark times?